D1299567

Marion Public Library
1095 6th Avenue
Marion, IA 52302-3428
(319) 377-3412

The
Ghastly Dandies
Do the Classics

Ben Gibson

A division of Penguin Young Readers Group
Published by the Penguin Group
Penguin Group (USA) Inc., 345 Hudson Street
New York, New York 10014, U.S.A.

USA / Canada / UK / Ireland / Australia / New Zealand / India / South Africa / China
Penguin Books Ltd, Registered Offices: 80 Strand, London WC2R 0RL, England
For more information about the Penguin Group visit penguin.com

Published simultaneously in Canada

Library of Congress Cataloging-in-Publication Data is available.

ISBN: 978-1-59514-527-7

Printed in the United States of America

1 3 5 7 9 10 8 6 4 2

ALWAYS LEARNING   PEARSON

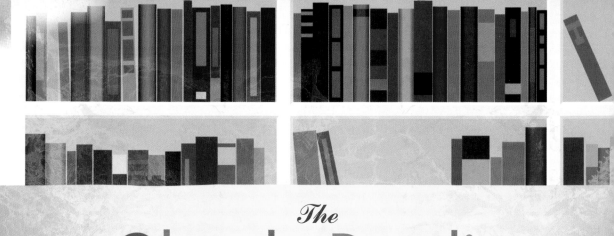

The
Ghastly Dandies
Do the Classics

······················

Ben Gibson

razOr
bill

An Imprint of Penguin Group (USA)

Greetings and salutations, dear readers!

I am pleased to introduce these classic tales, as told by the Ghastly Dandies.

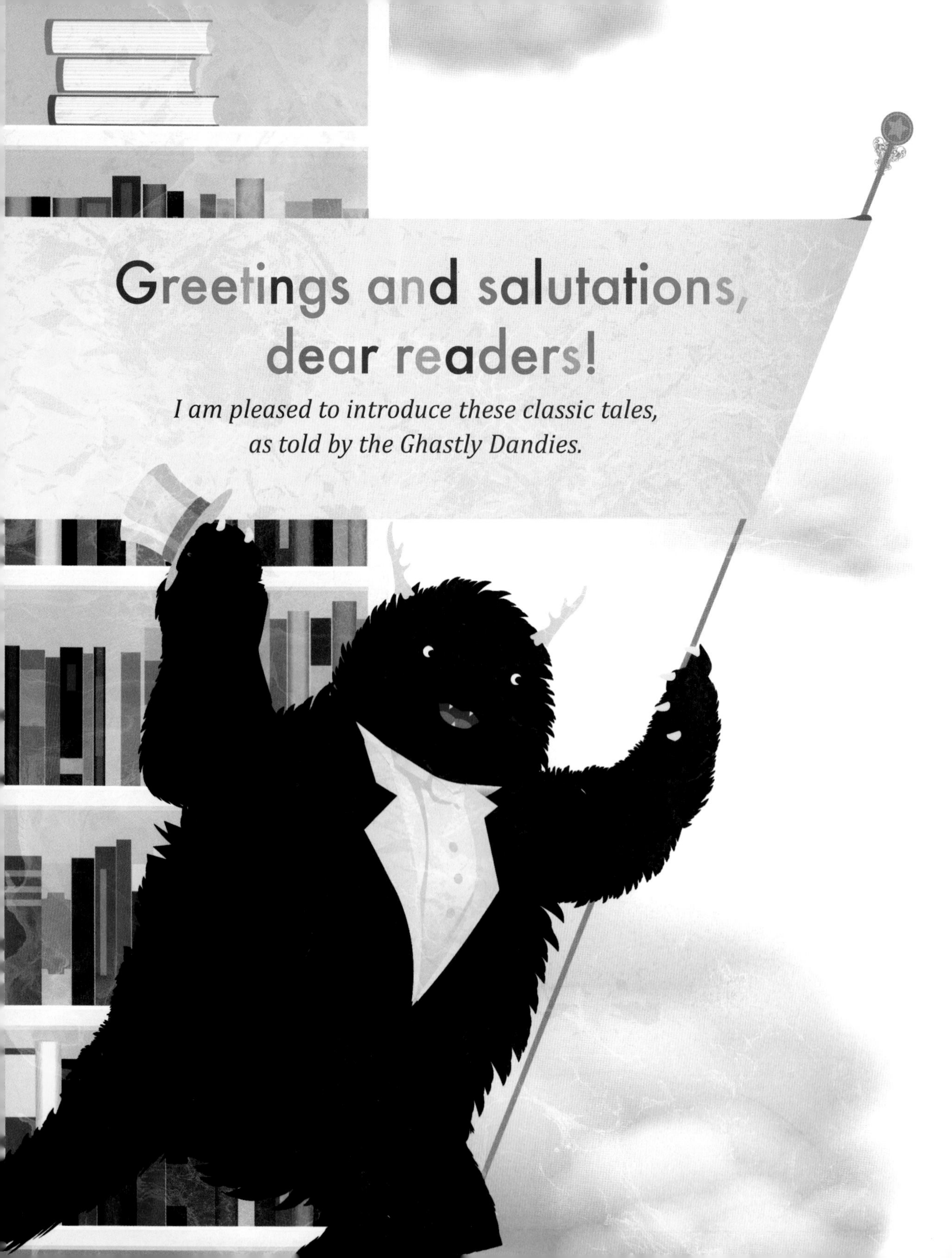

DON
QUIXOTE

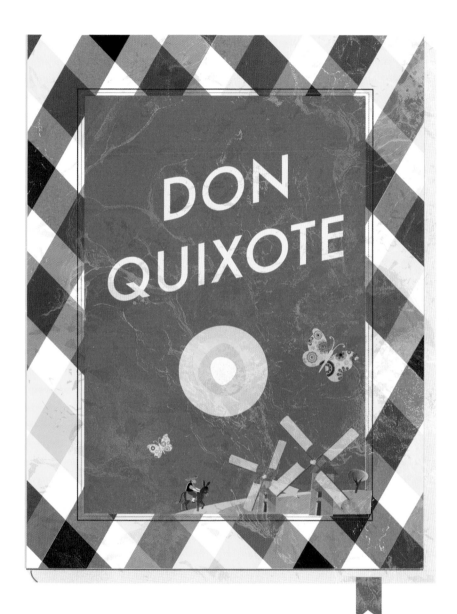

In a very old house, in a very old village somewhere in La Mancha, there once lived a Dandy named Alonso who loved to read.

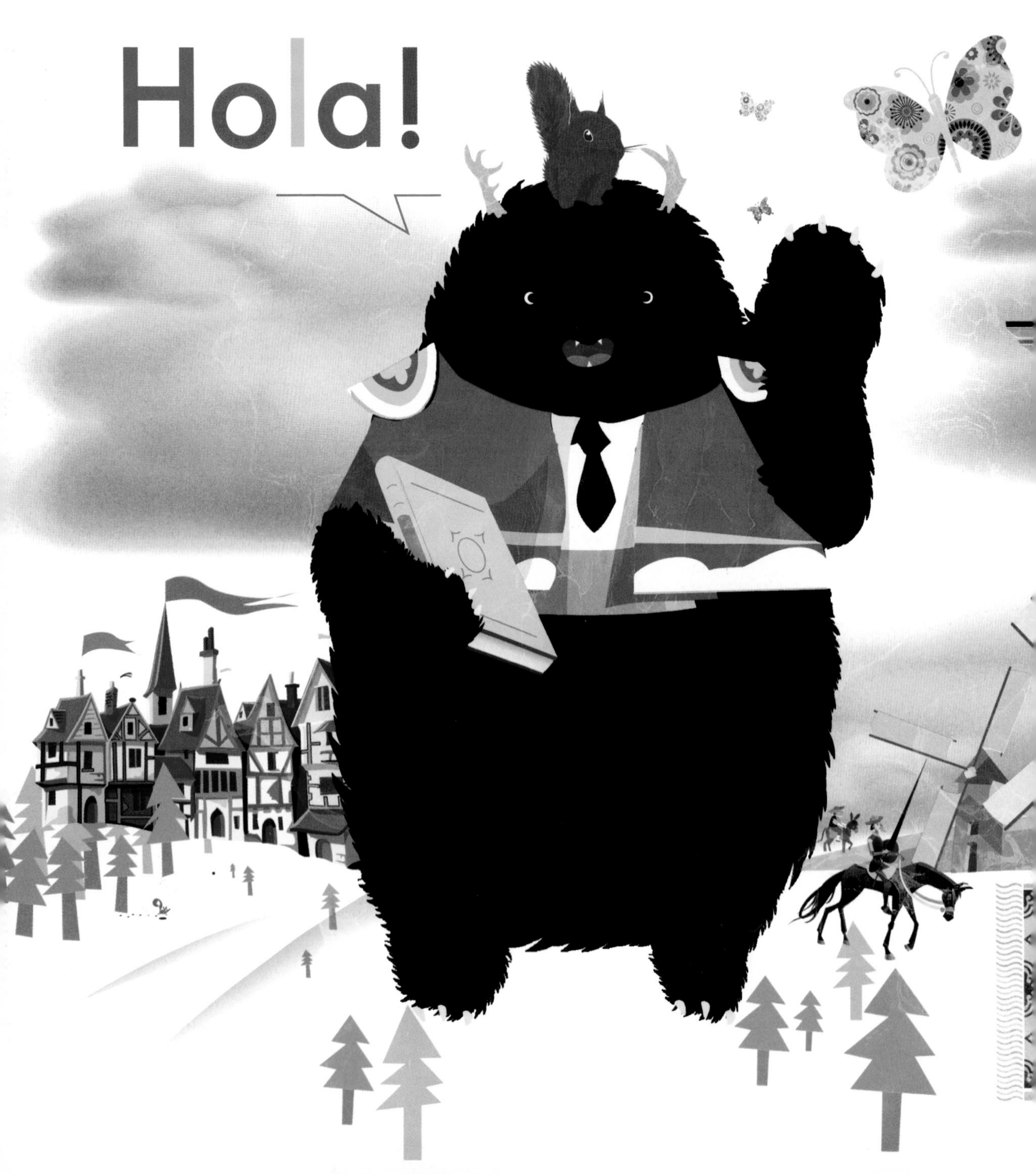
Hola!

But his niece, Antonia, worried that he spent too much time in his imagination.

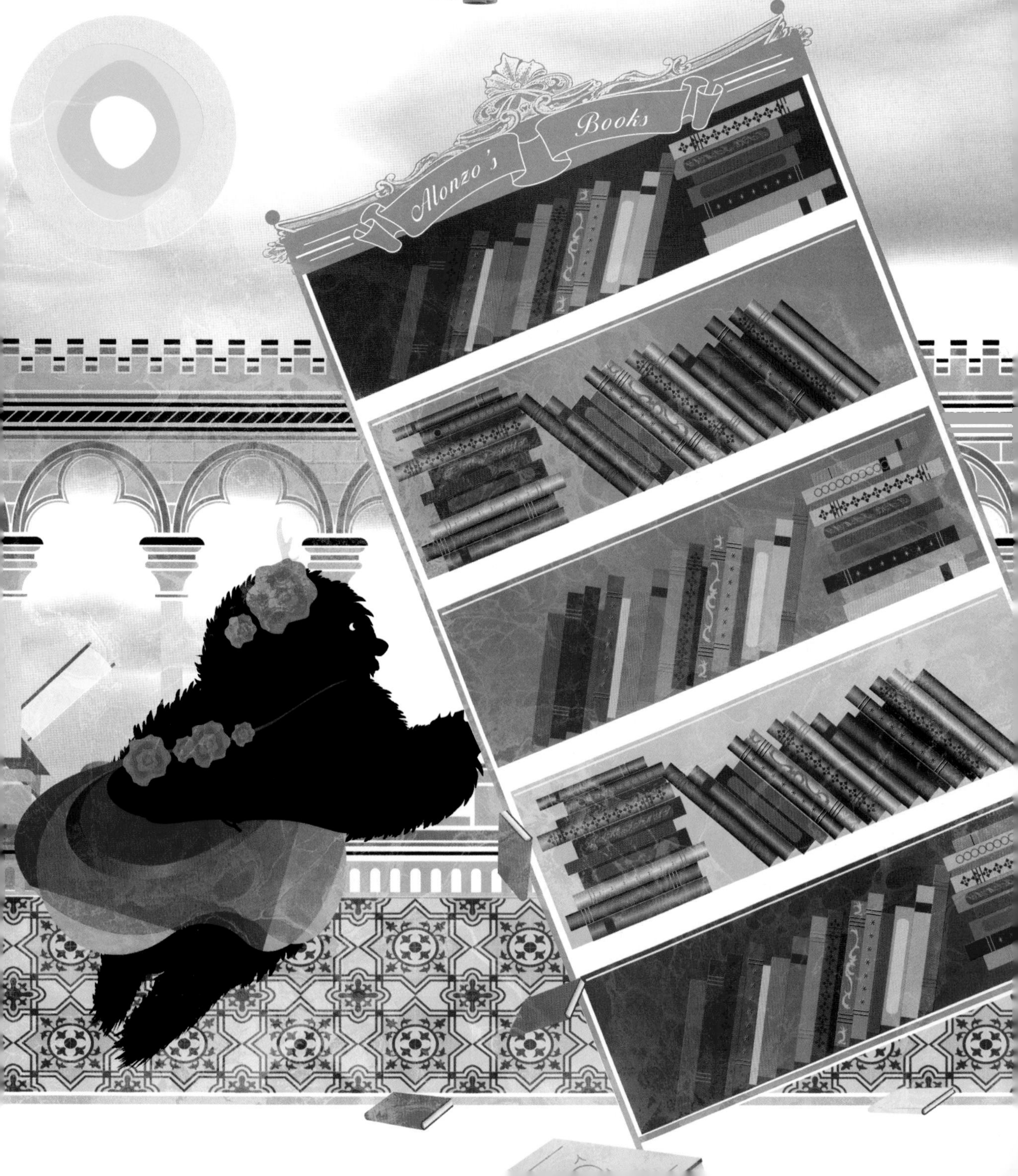
Alonzo's Books

So Alonso found an old suit of armor and flew off into the countryside with his friend, Sancho . . .

I am Don Quixote de la Mancha!

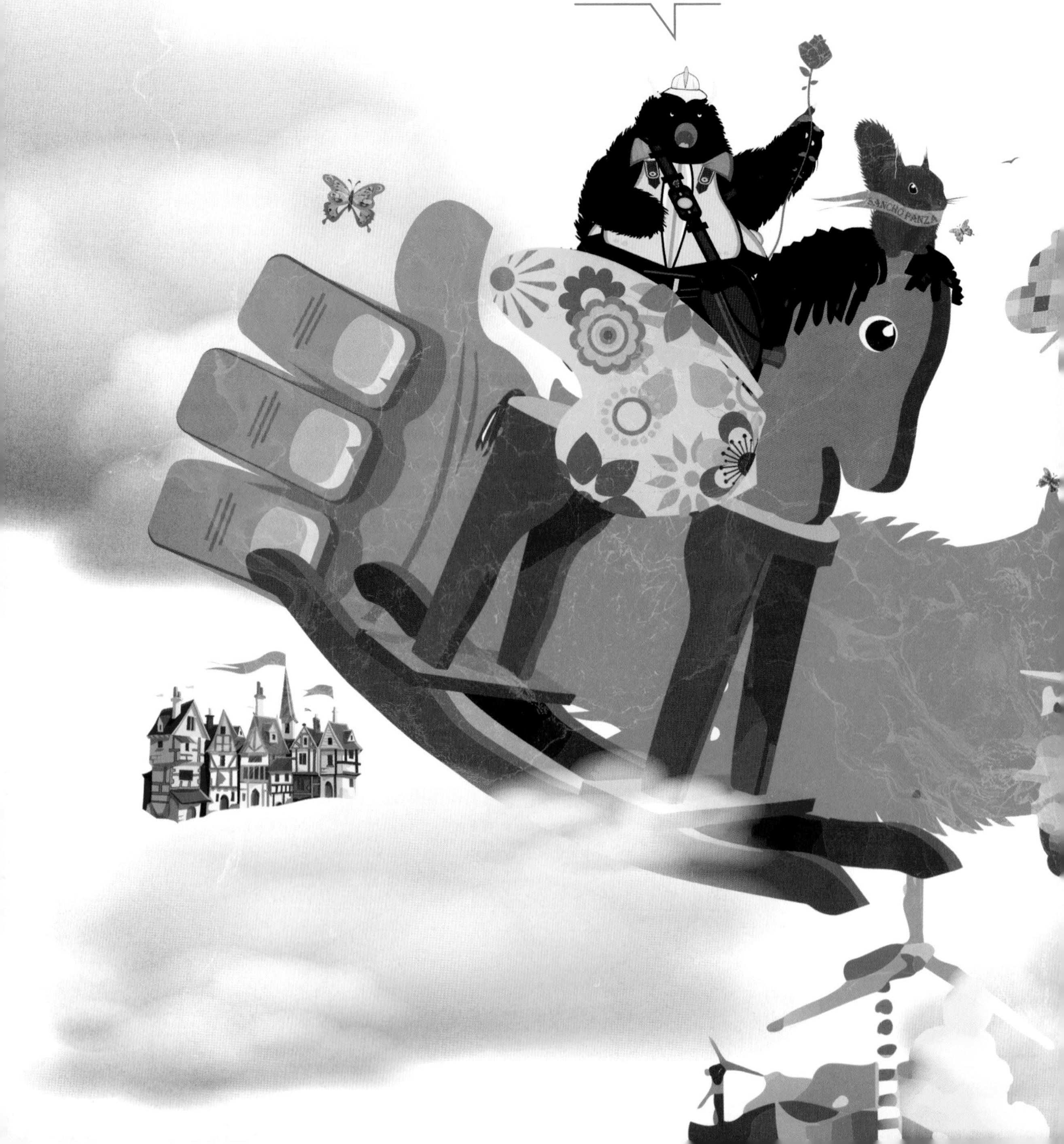

SANCHO PANZA

. . . but the countryside was guarded by ferocious giants.

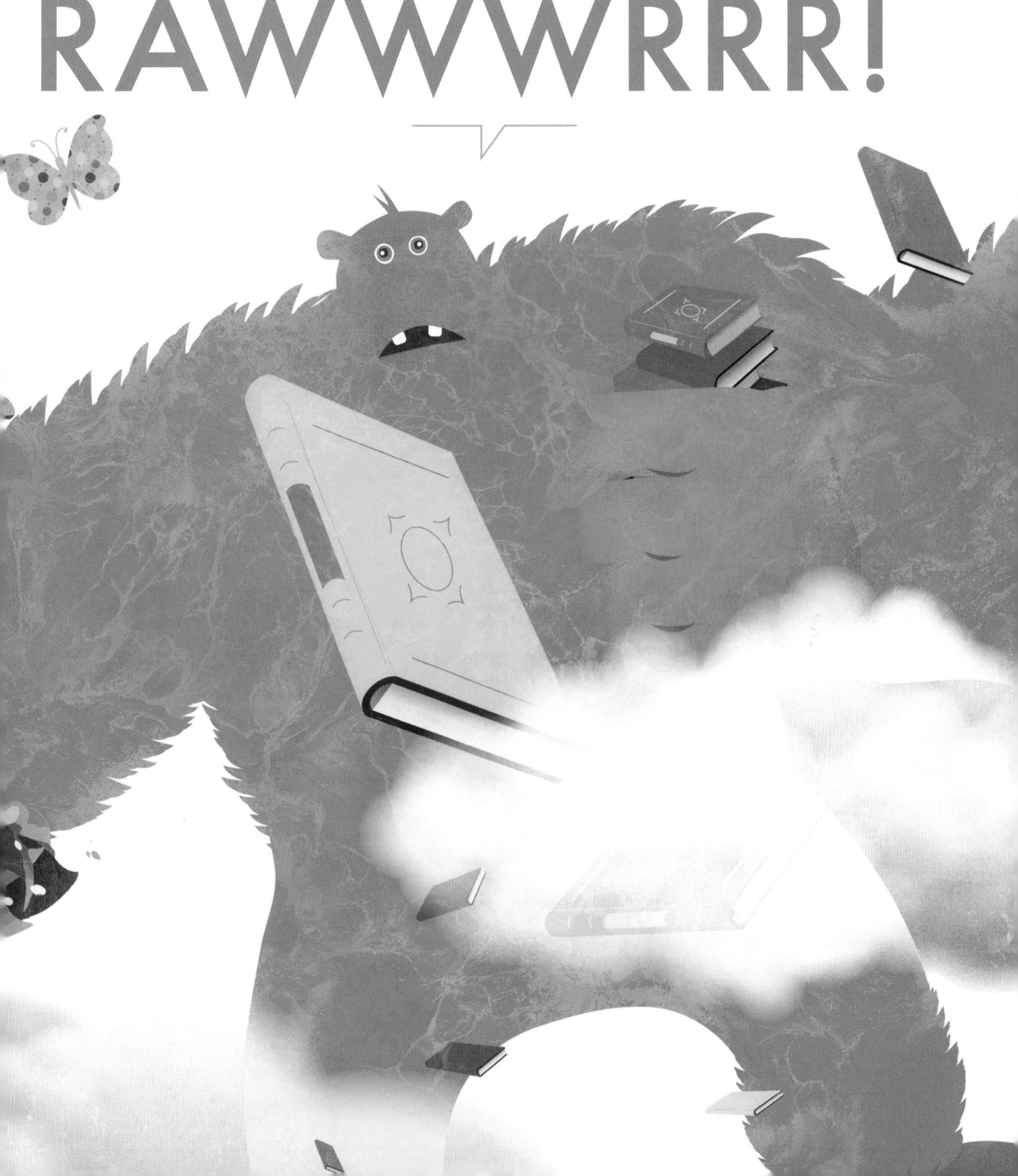
RAWWWRRR!

The giants were a little too scary, so Don Quixote flew away again and became the ruler of a magical island.

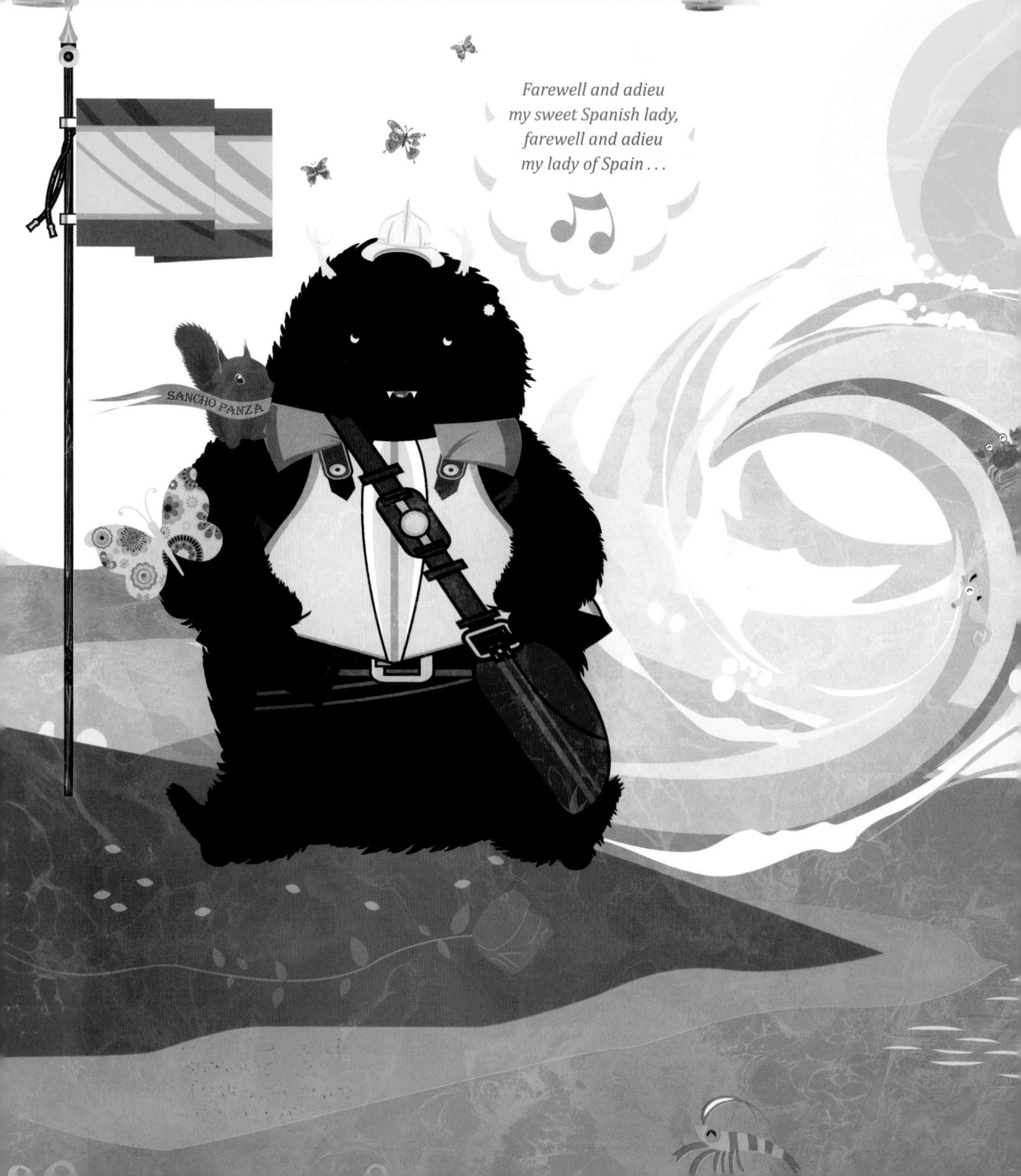
Farewell and adieu
my sweet Spanish lady,
farewell and adieu
my lady of Spain . . .
SANCHO PANZA

After spending some time on the island, though,
Don Quixote grew very lonely, and very hungry.
Luckily, his niece sent villagers to rescue him.

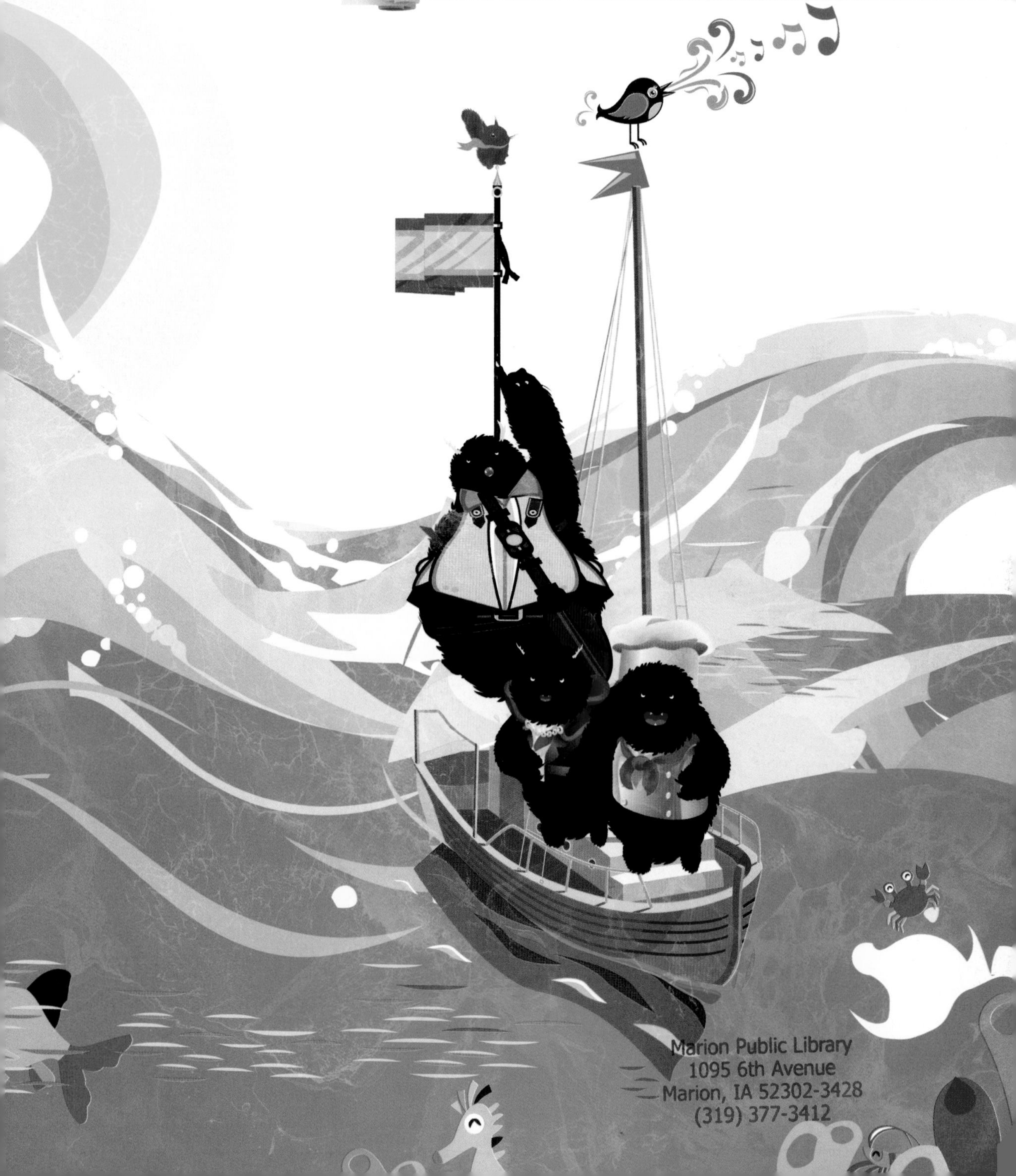

And so Alonso returned home, where he had a nice supper and read one story before bed.

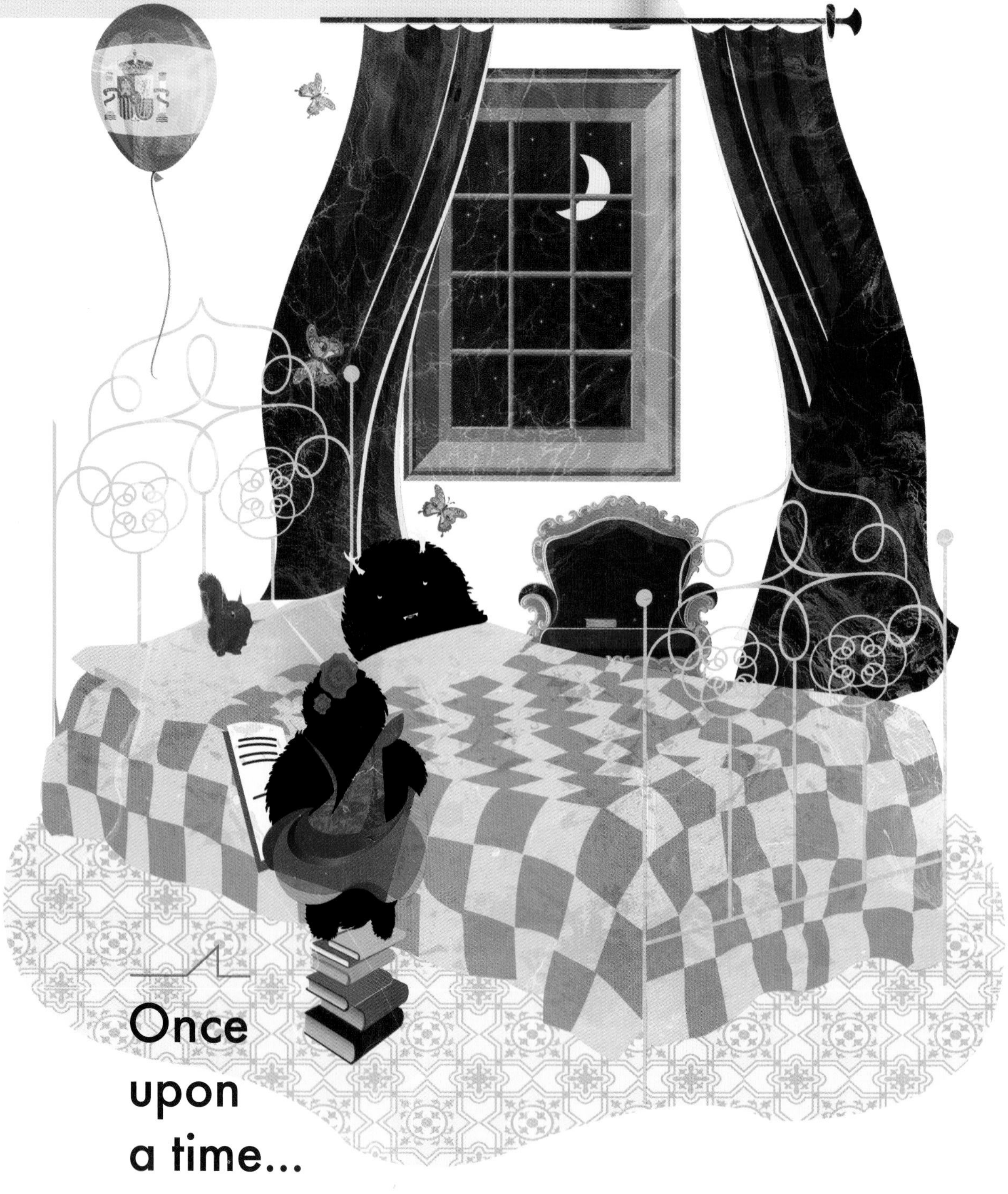

Once upon a time...

FRANKENSTEIN

Or, The Modern Prometheus

When he was a very young Dandy, Victor Frankenstein decided that when he grew up, he would become a scientist . . .

I will in thi

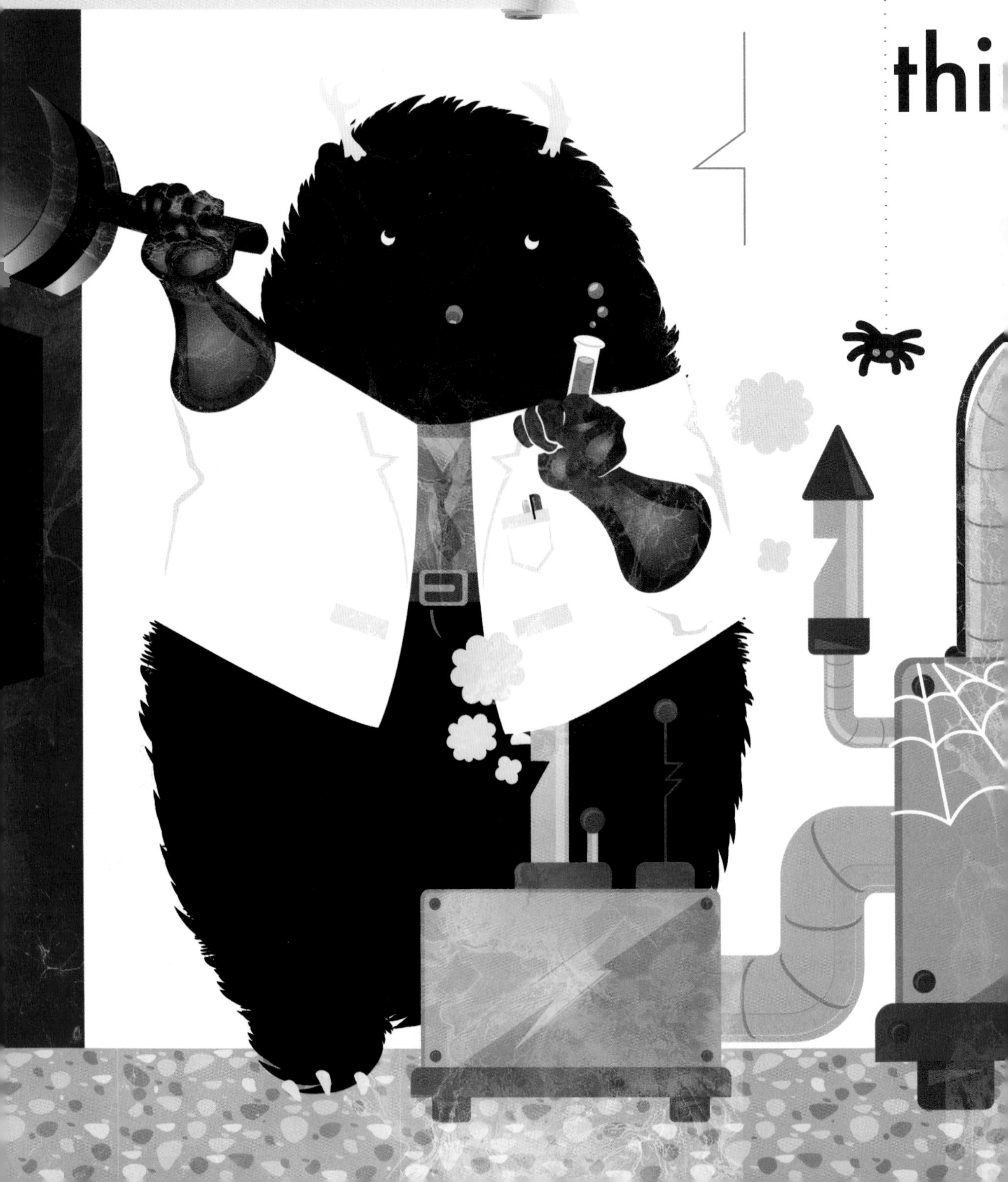

ent the greatest
g the world has
ever seen!

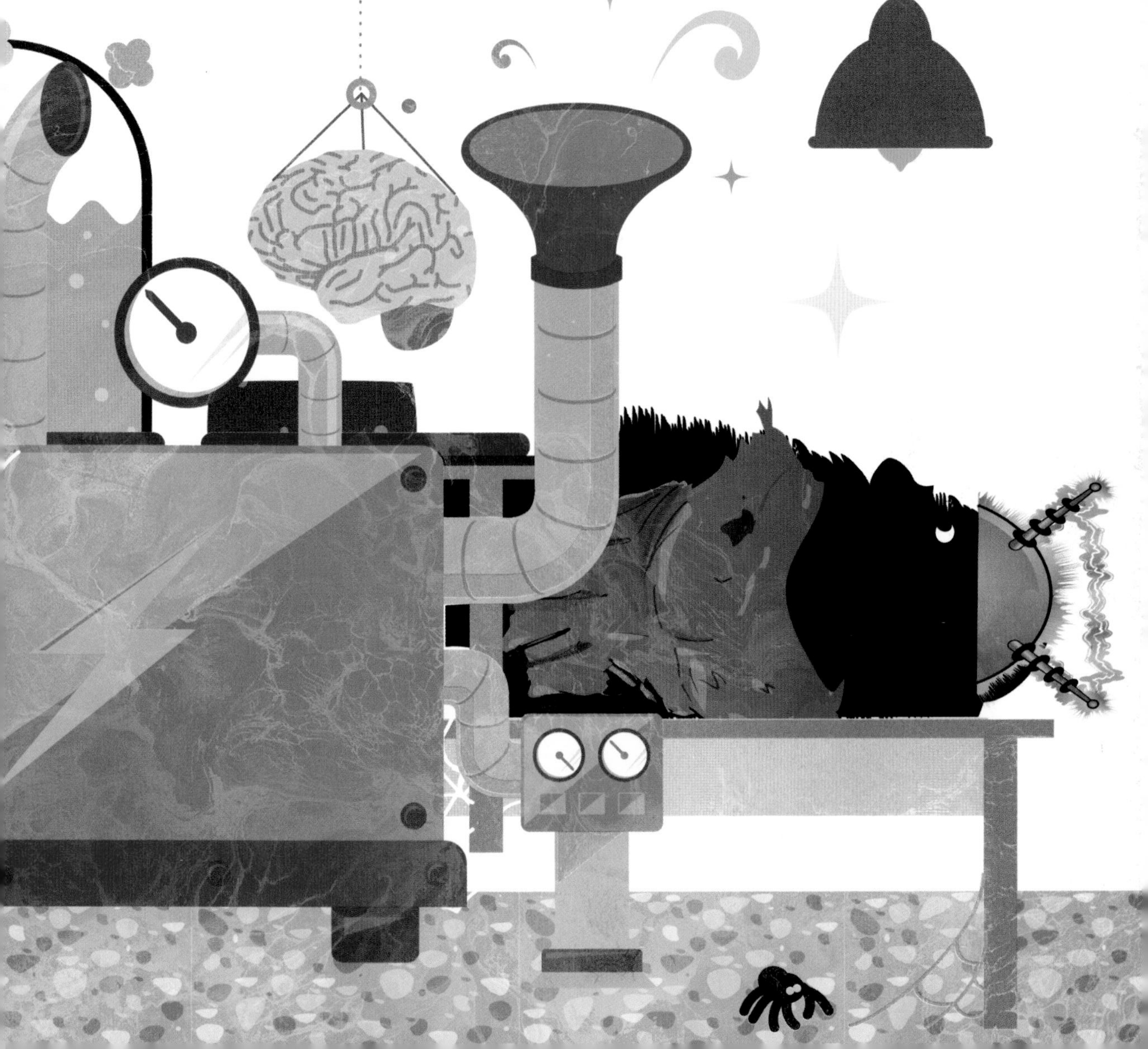

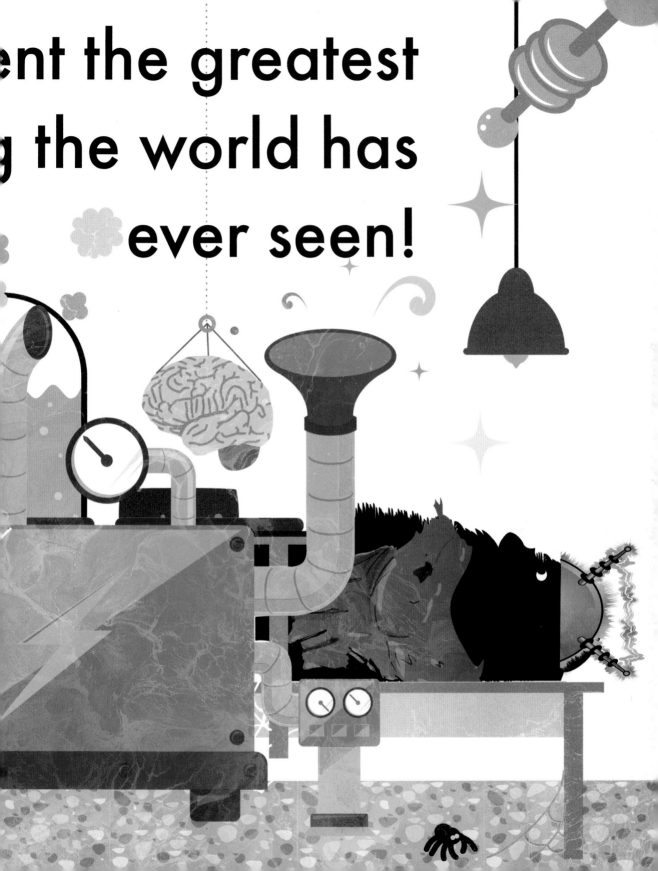

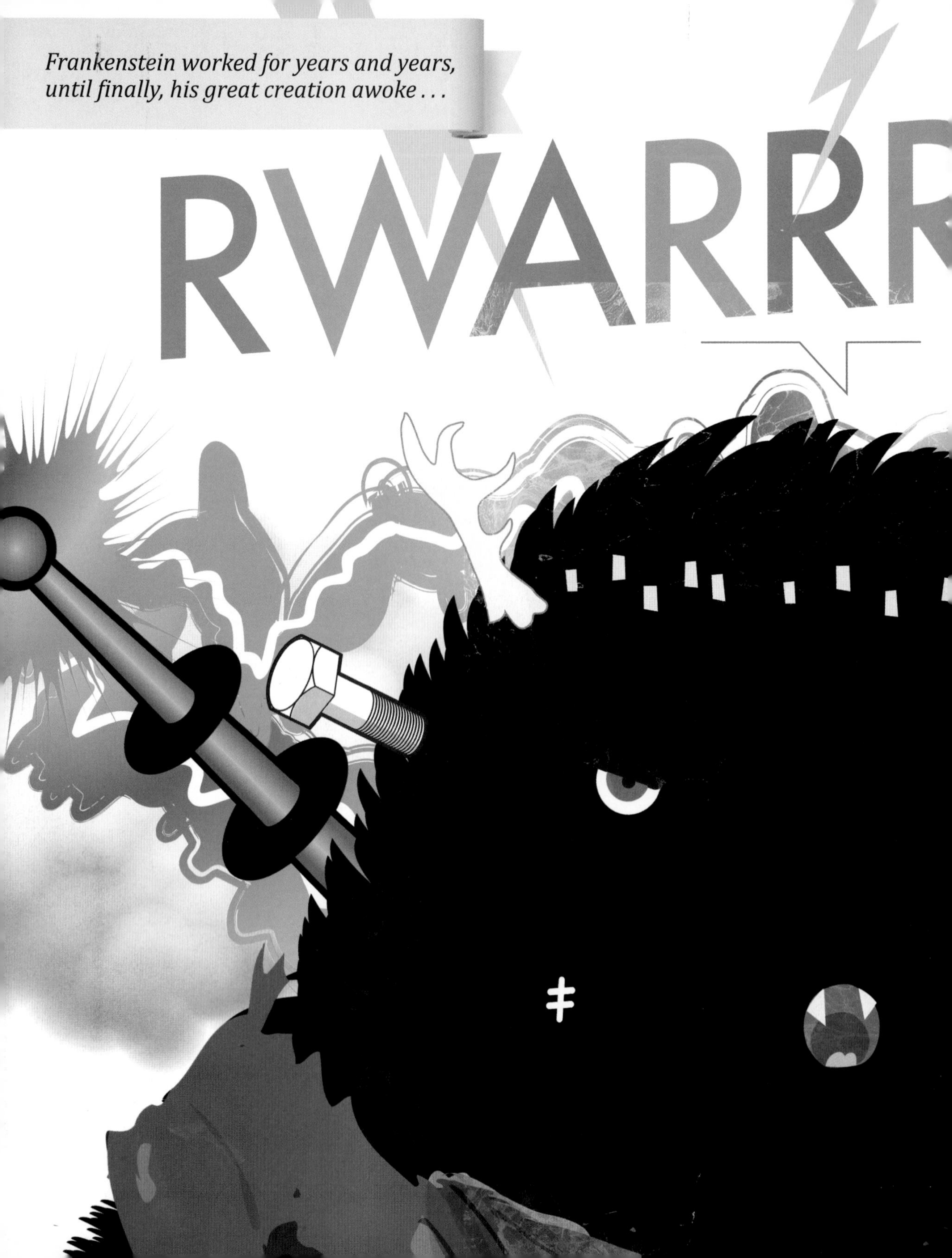
Frankenstein worked for years and years, until finally, his great creation awoke . . .
RWARRR

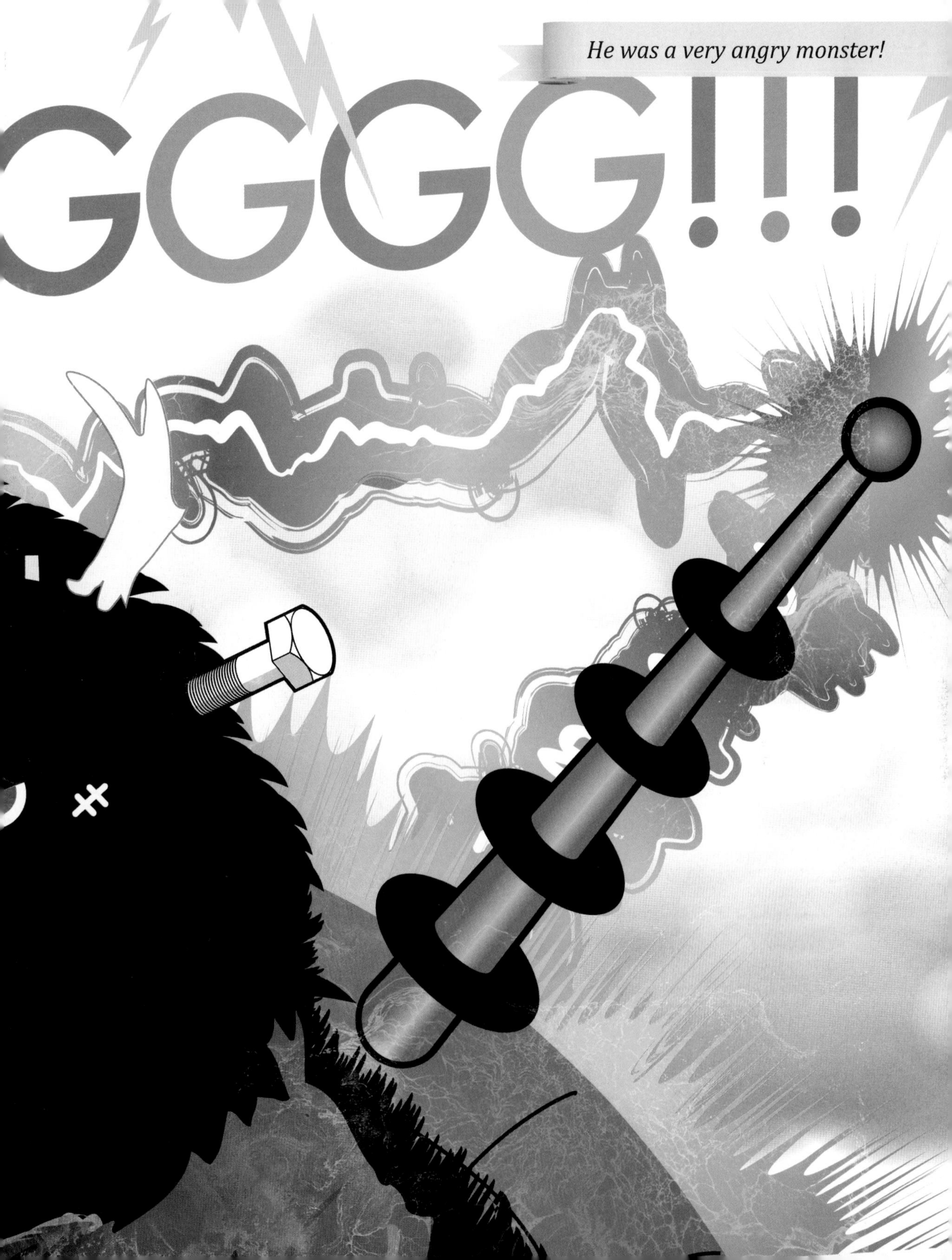
He was a very angry monster!
GGGG!!!

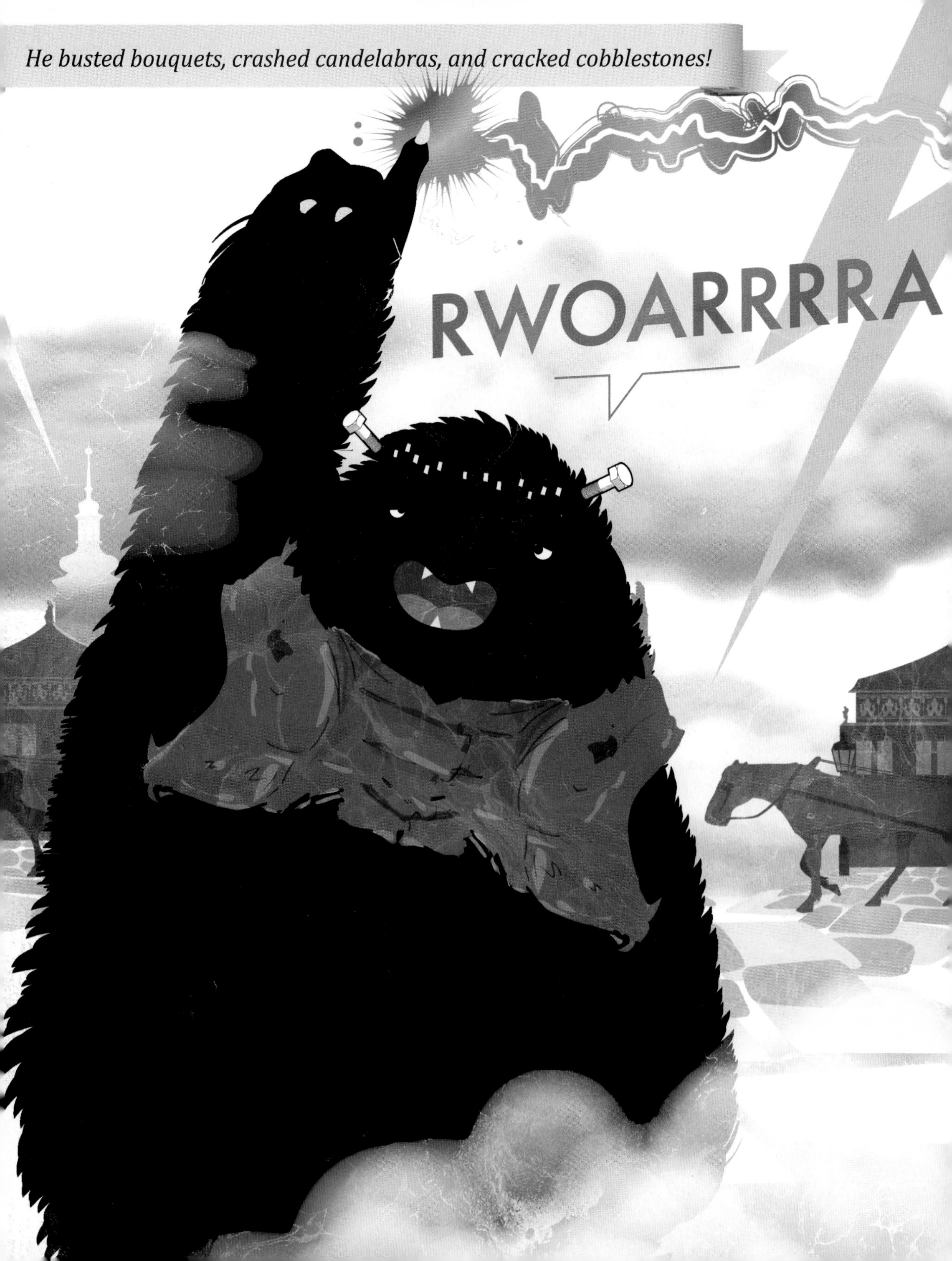
He busted bouquets, crashed candelabras, and cracked cobblestones!
RWOARRRRA

The neighbors became fed up and chased Victor's monster away.

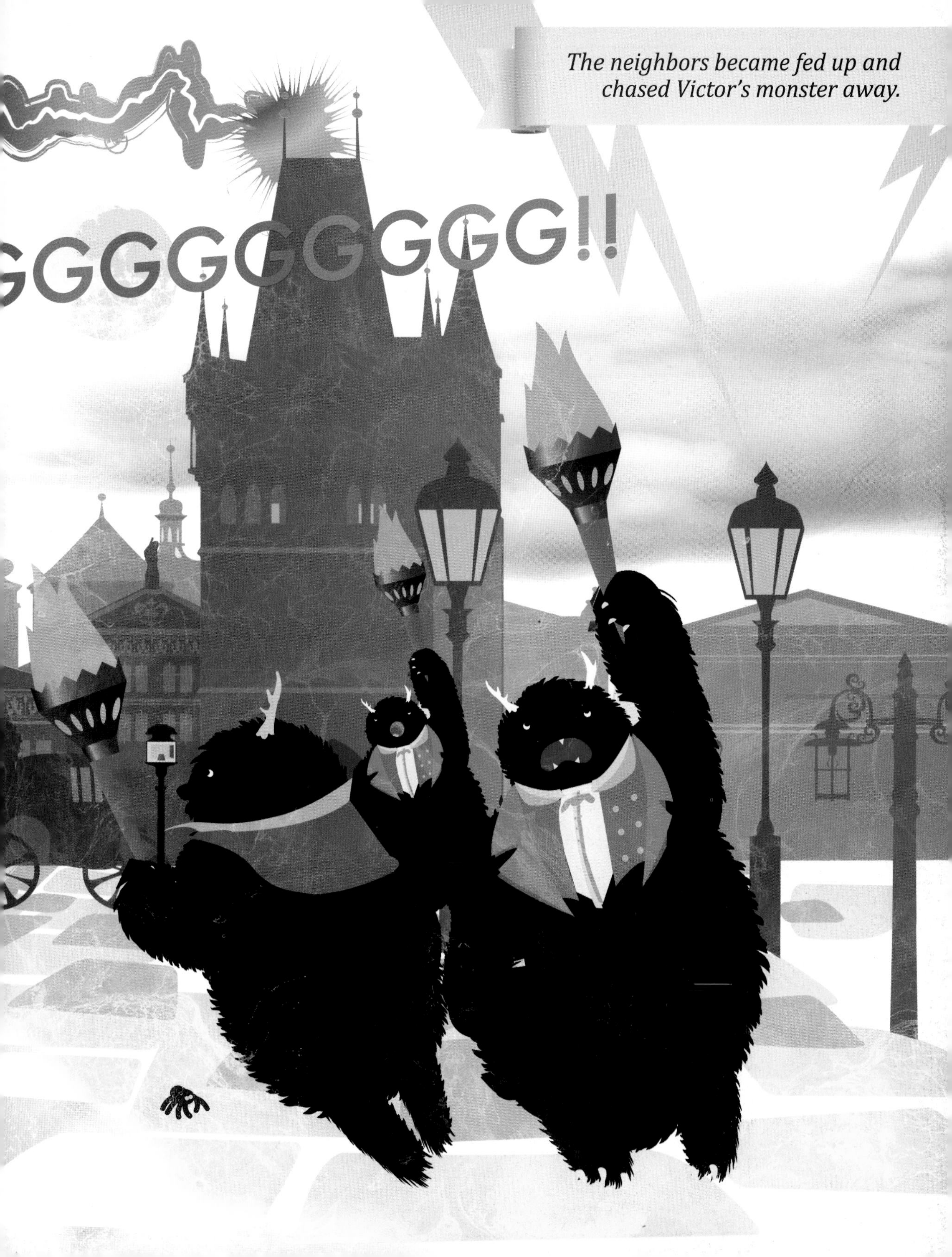
GGGGGGGGG!!

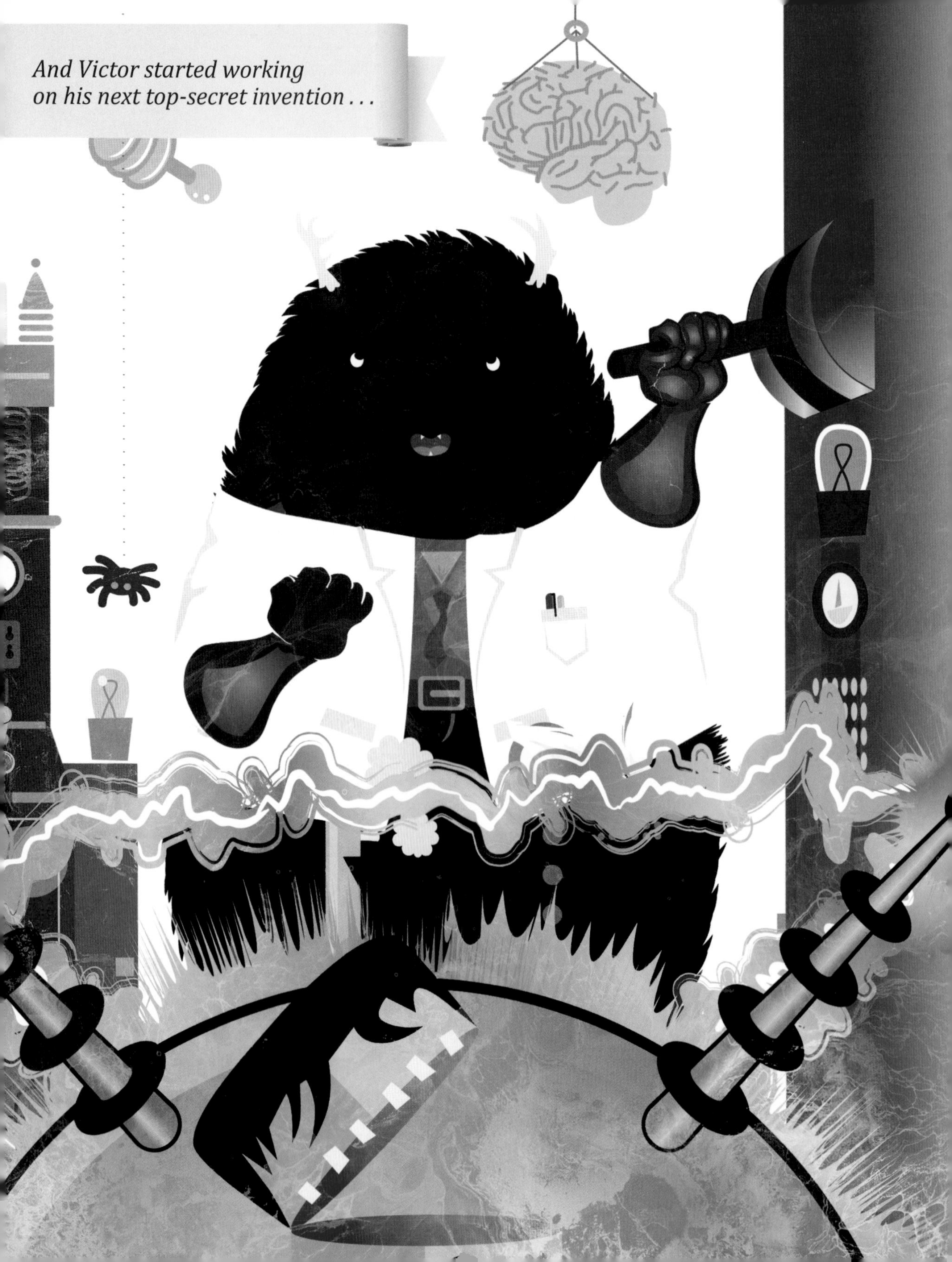
And Victor started working on his next top-secret invention . . .

The
GREAT
GATSBY

One summer, Nick's family moved to the lovely town of West Egg.

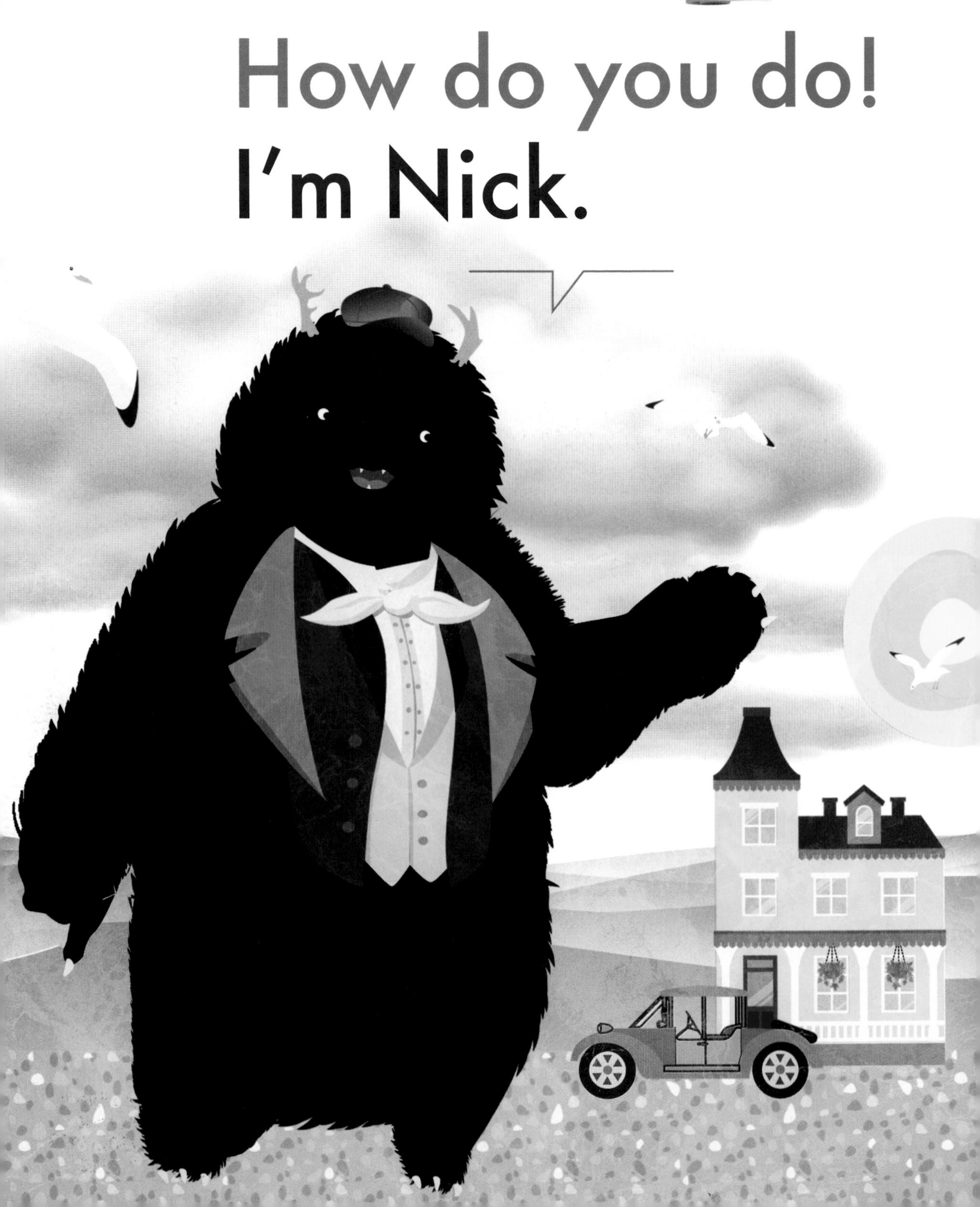
How do you do!
I'm Nick.

There was a humongous house next door that belonged to a Dandy named Gatsby.

Salutations! **I'd love it if you attended a party with Daisy and me!**

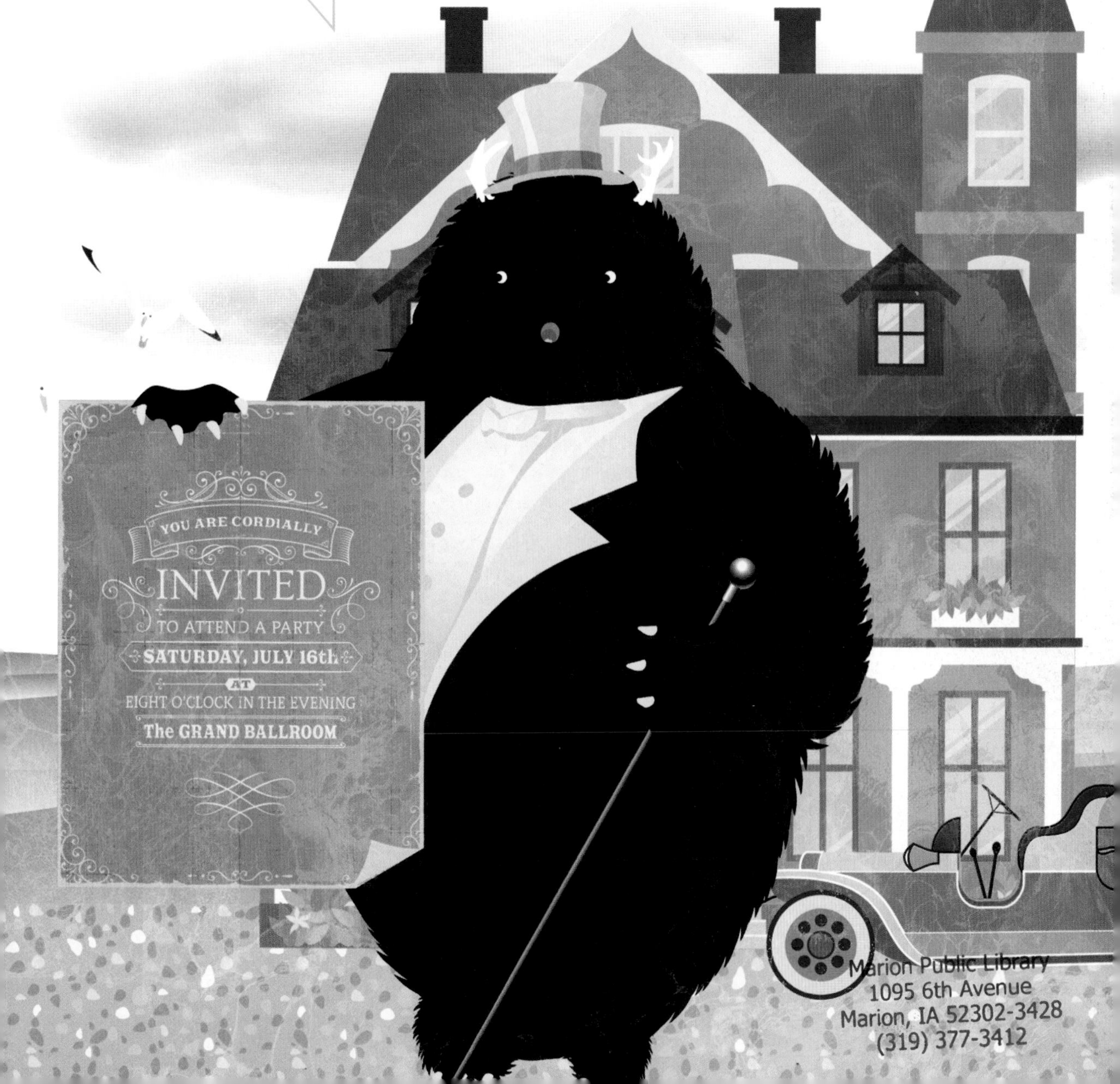
YOU ARE CORDIALLY
INVITED
TO ATTEND A PARTY
SATURDAY, JULY 16th
AT
EIGHT O'CLOCK IN THE EVENING
The GRAND BALLROOM

Gatsby was quite a Dandy! He had the finest things!

Pink champagne and pearl necklaces!

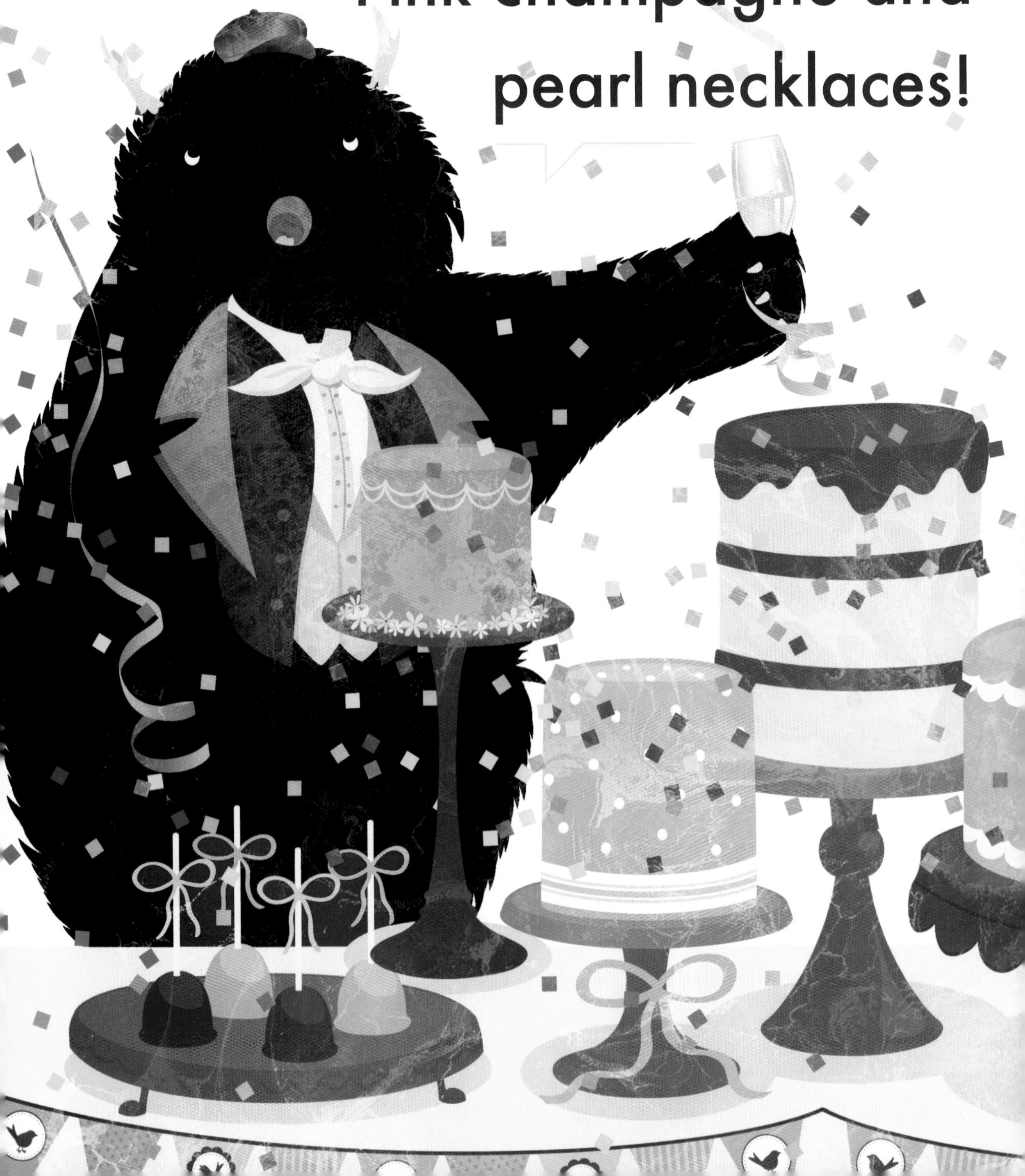

Caviar and crumb cakes!

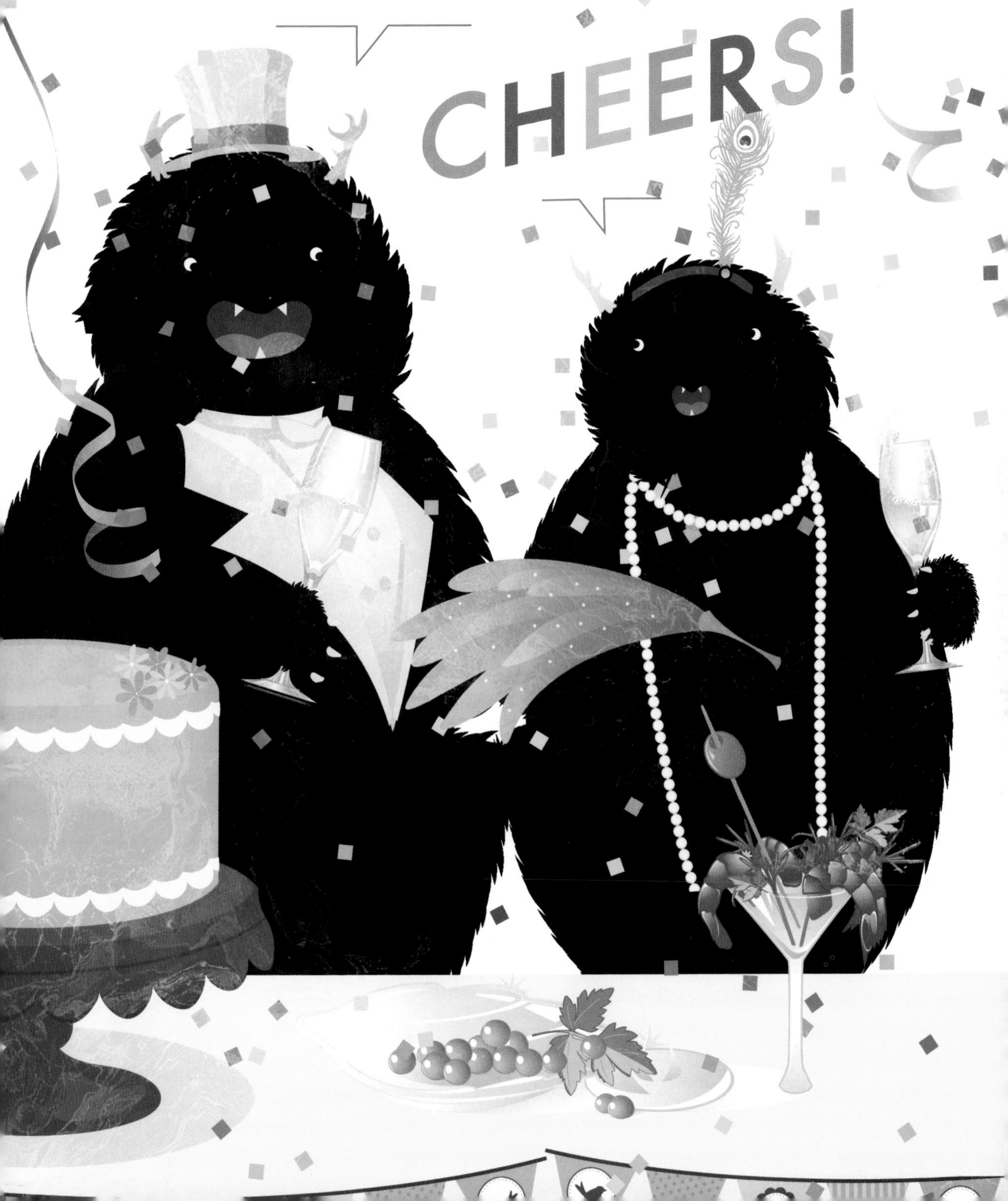
CHEERS!

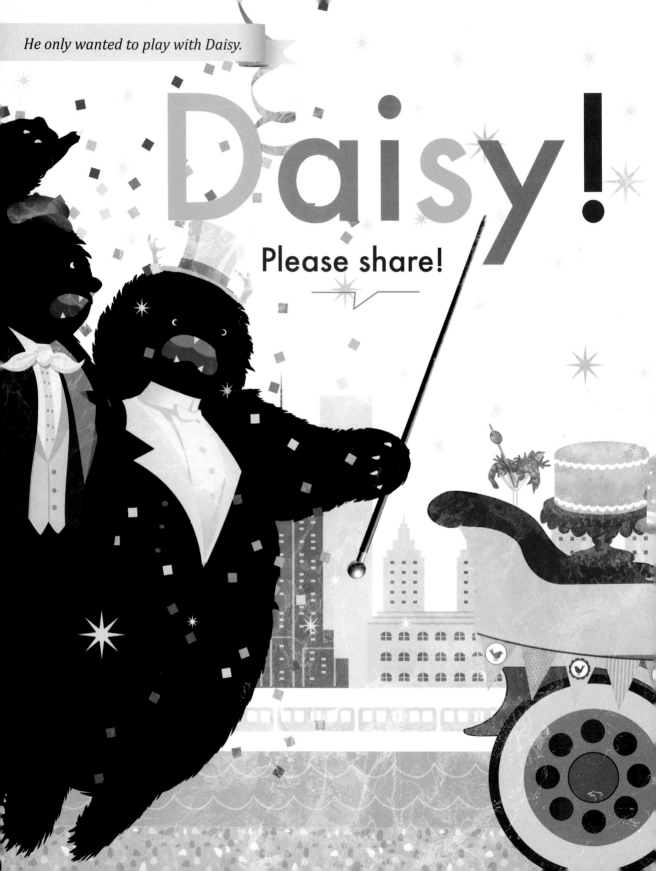

He only wanted to play with Daisy.

Daisy!

Please share!

Daisy had other plans, though, which made everyone very sad . . .

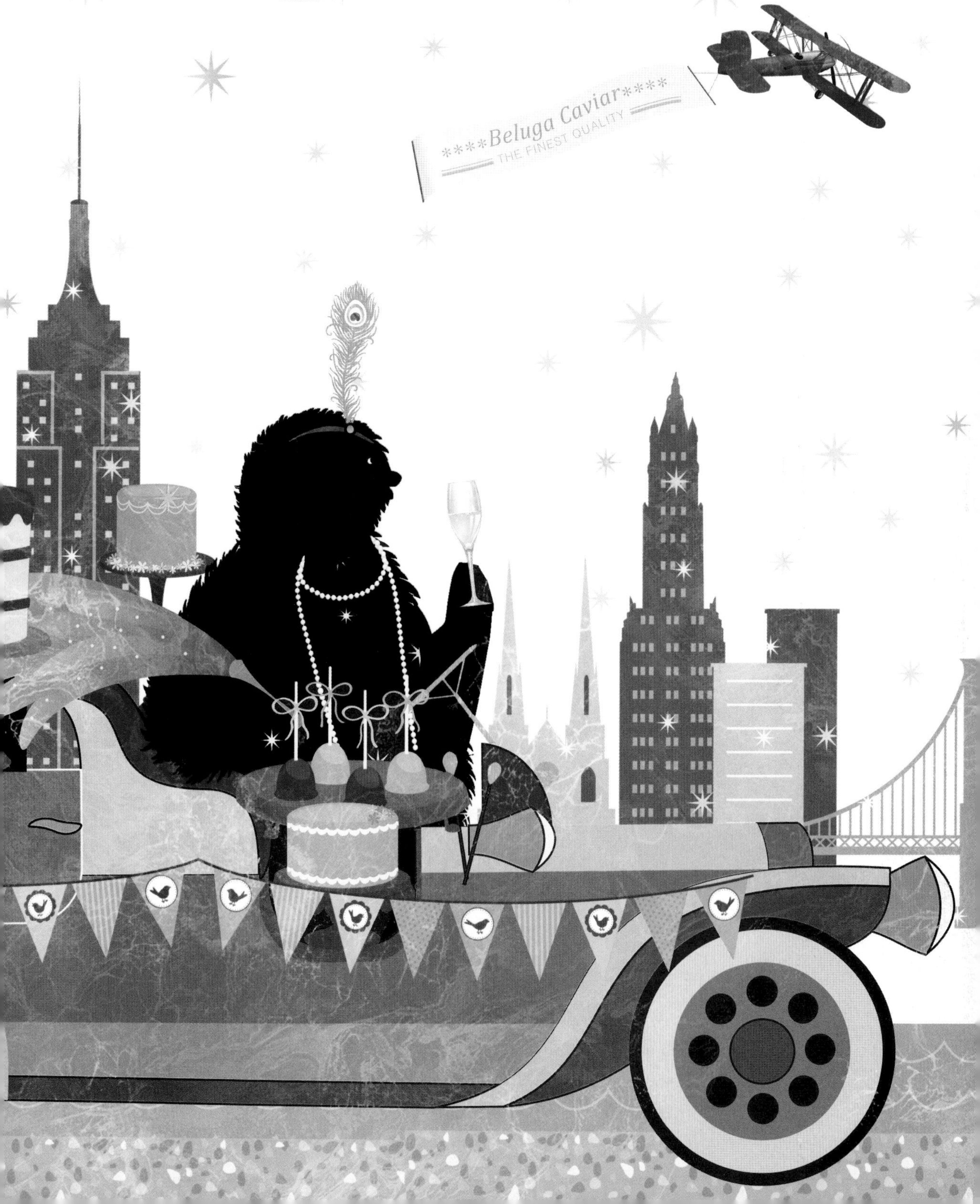
****Beluga Caviar****
THE FINEST QUALITY

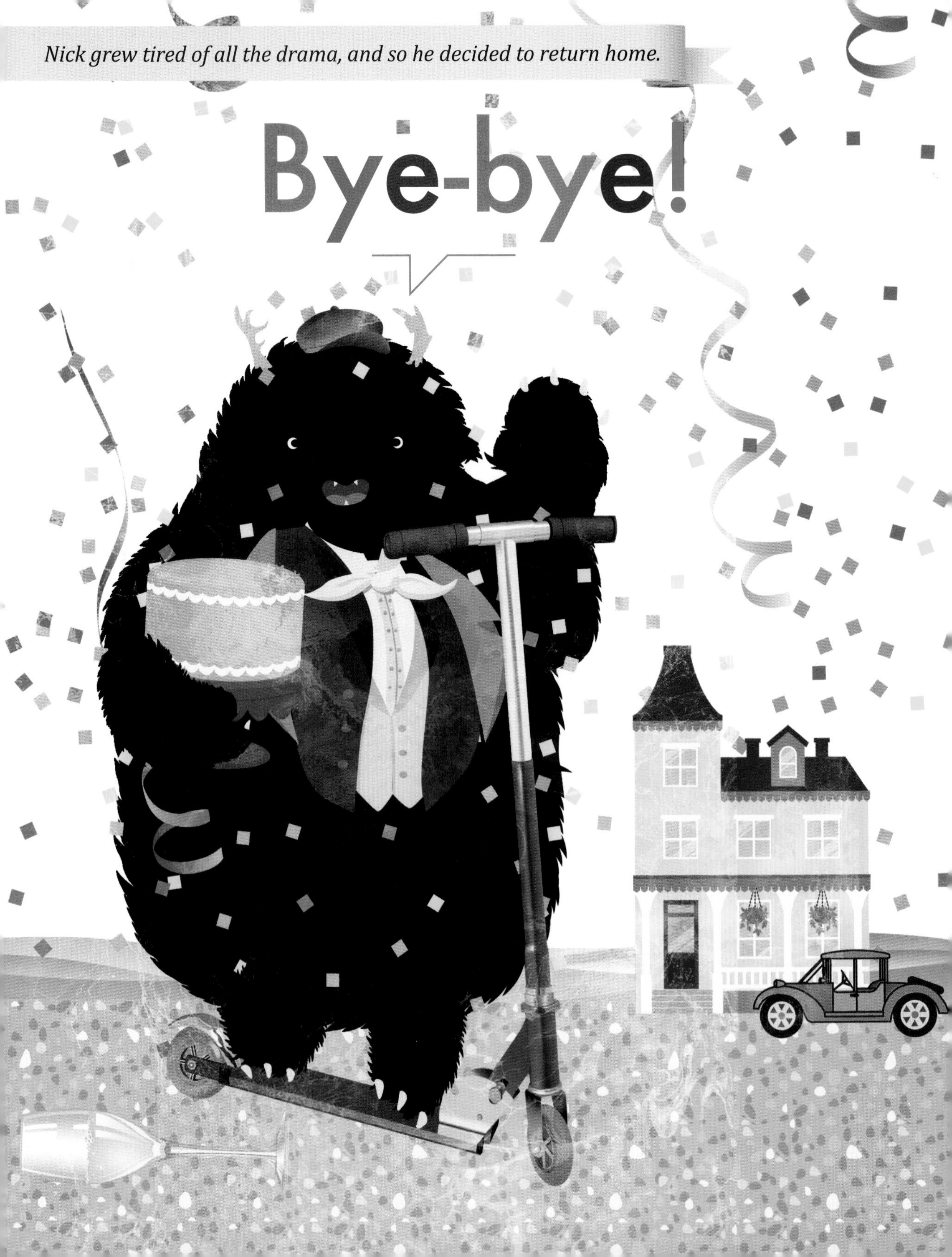
Nick grew tired of all the drama, and so he decided to return home.
Bye-bye!

MOBY
DICK
Or, The White Whale

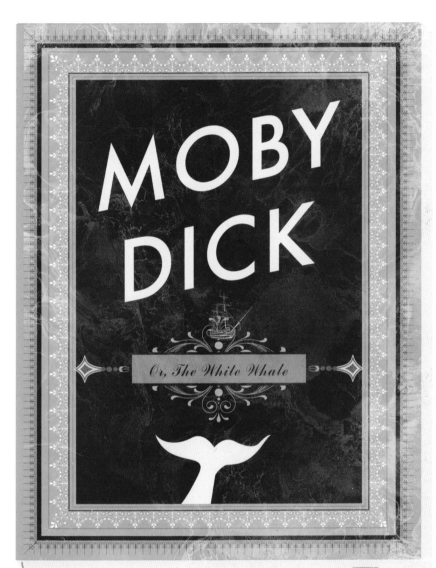

One stormy afternoon, Ishmael was in the mood for adventure and decided to set sail with crabby Captain Ahab.

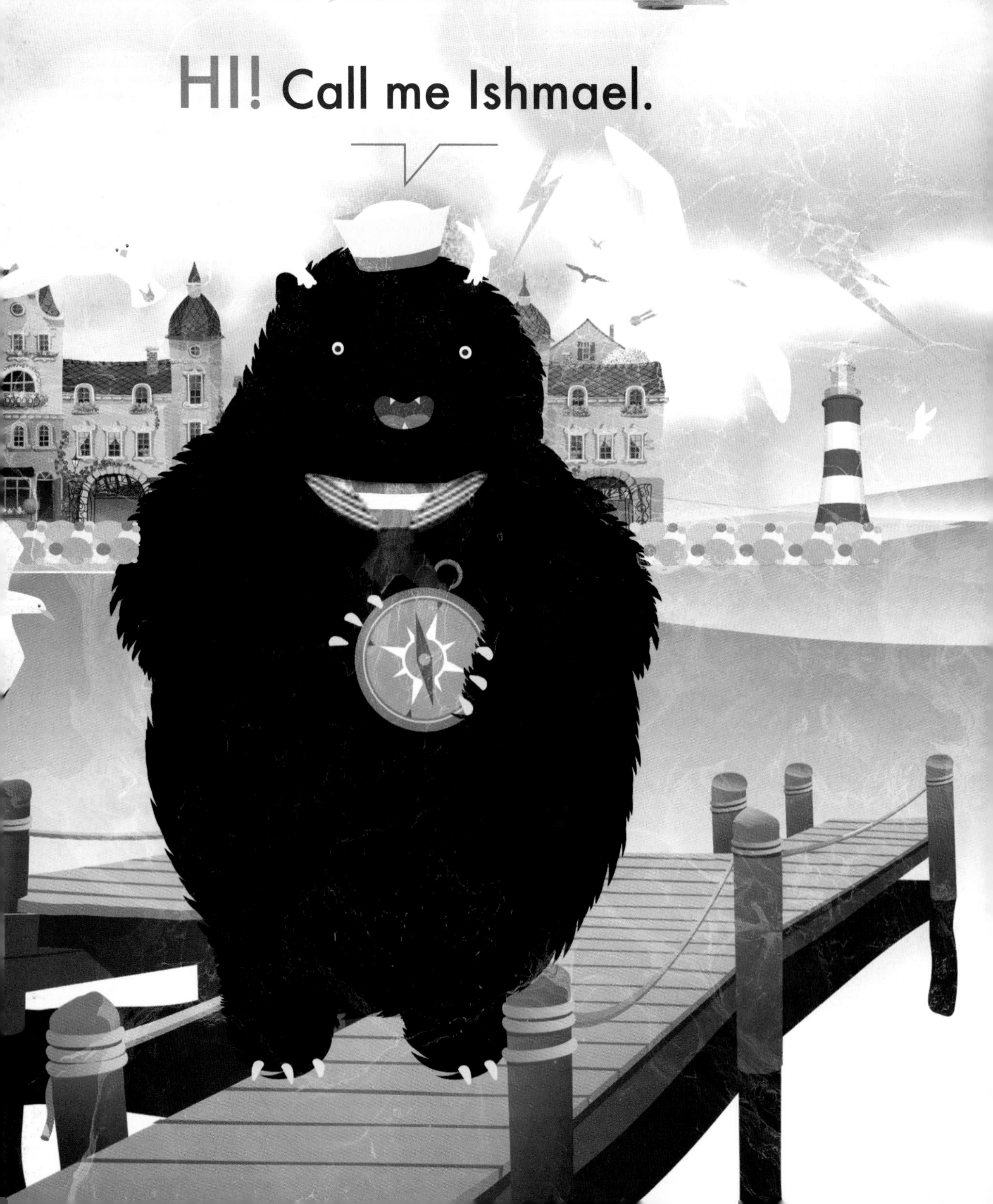
HI! Call me Ishmael.

Ahab had searched the seven seas for Moby Dick the whale, but to no avail.

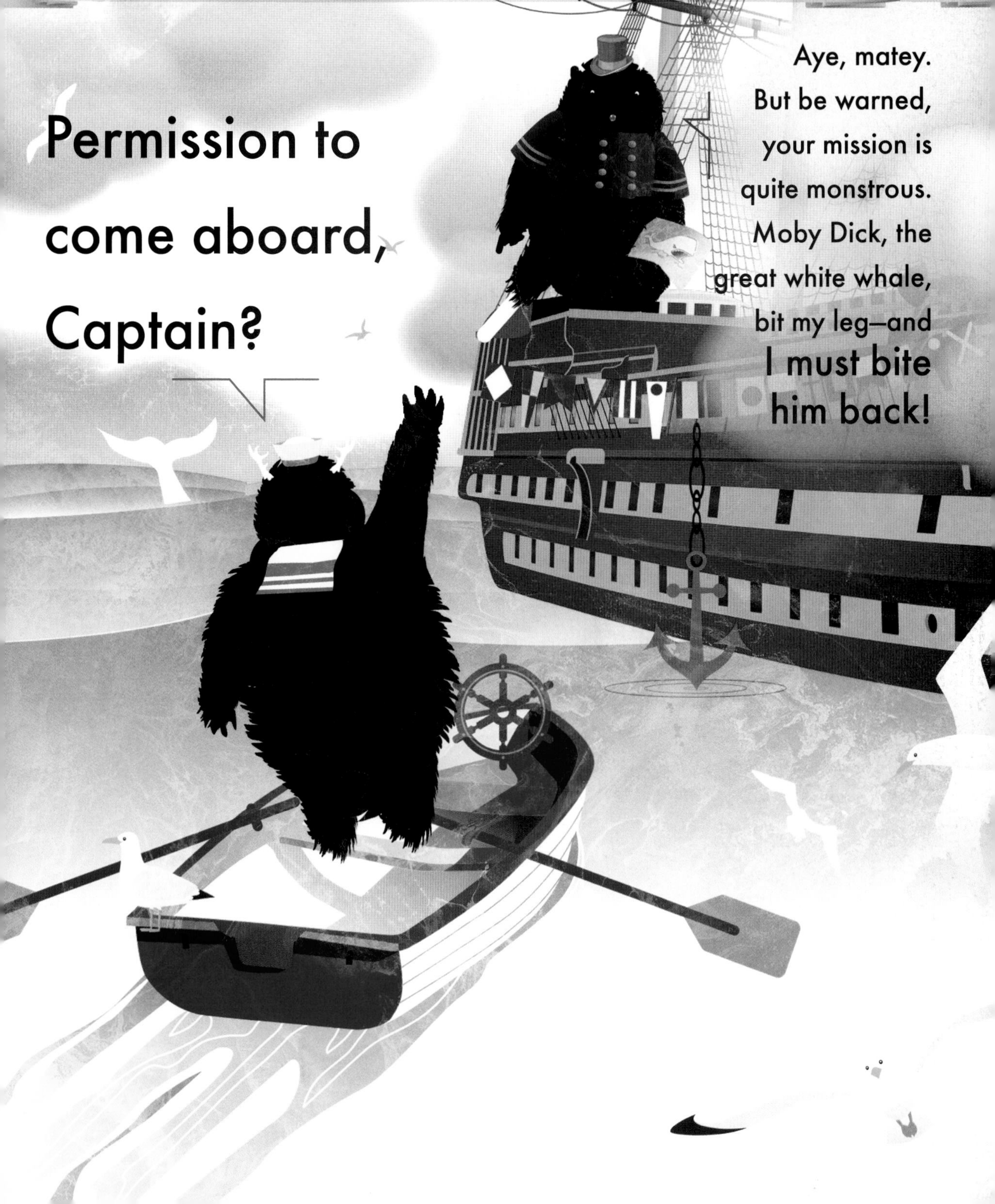
Permission to come aboard, Captain?
Aye, matey. But be warned, your mission is quite monstrous. Moby Dick, the great white whale, bit my leg—and I must bite him back!

Until that fateful day when they spied the great whale in the distance!

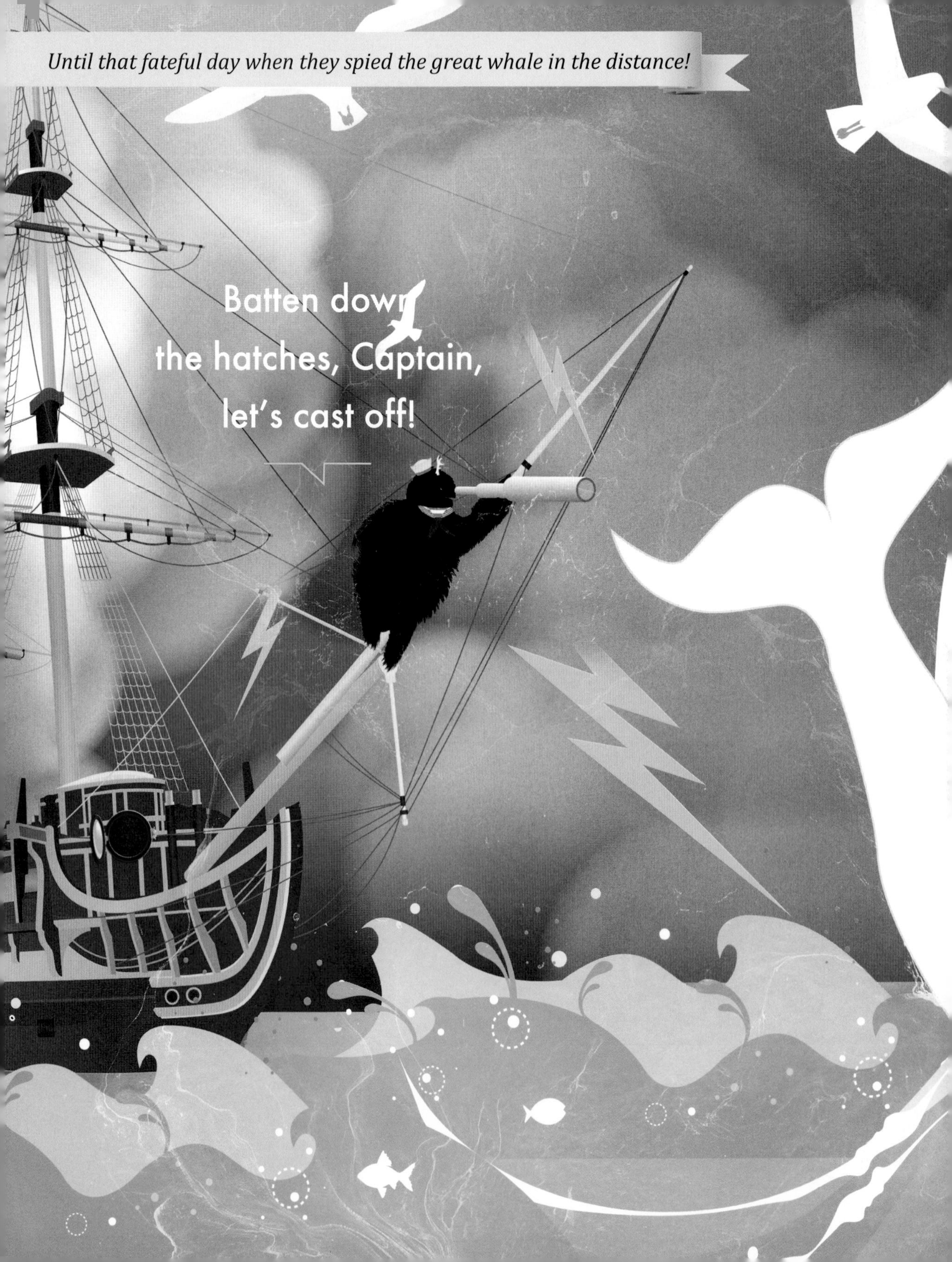
Batten down the hatches, Captain, let's cast off!

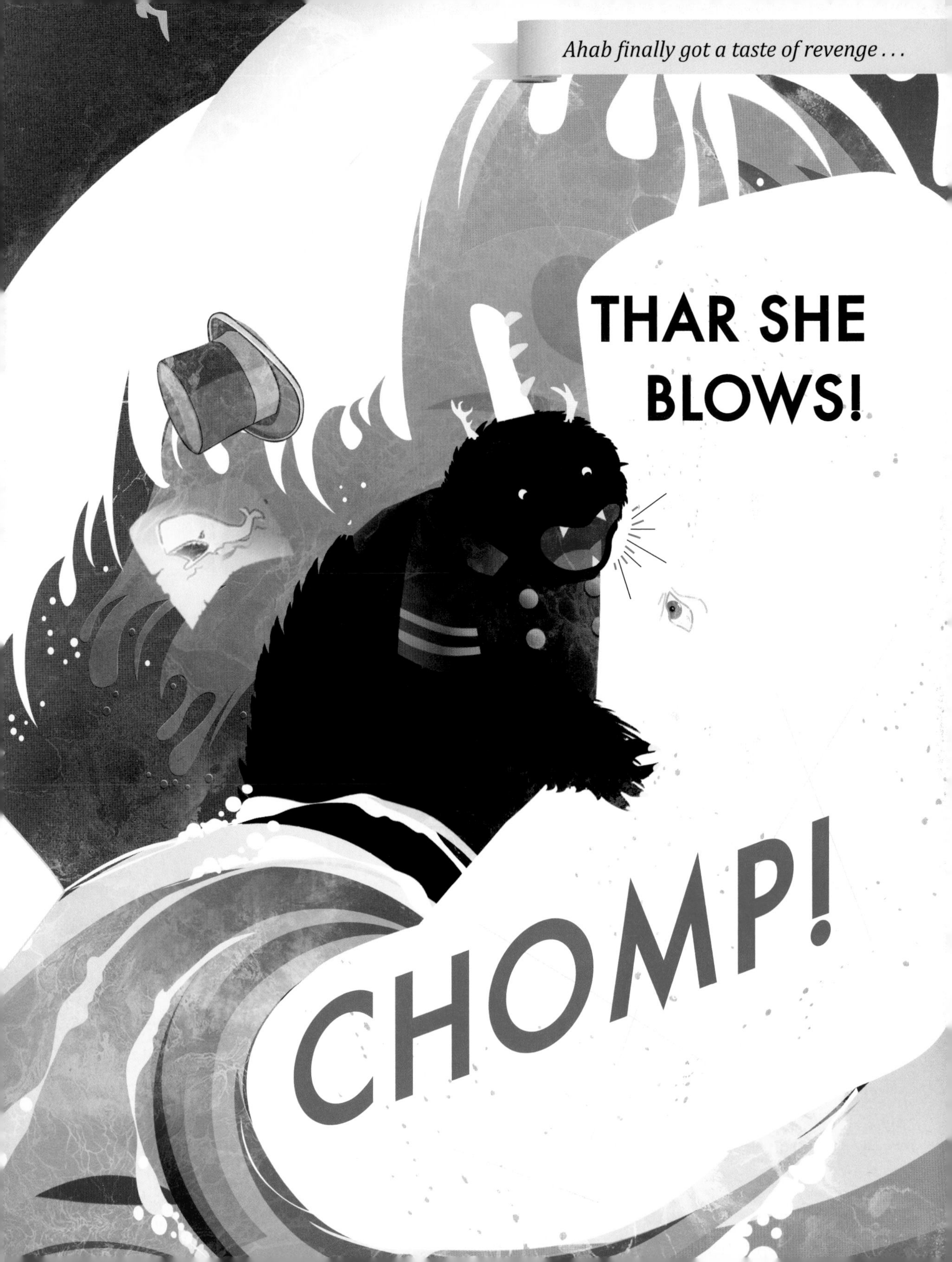
Ahab finally got a taste of revenge . . .
THAR SHE BLOWS!
CHOMP!

. . . but it tasted super gross.

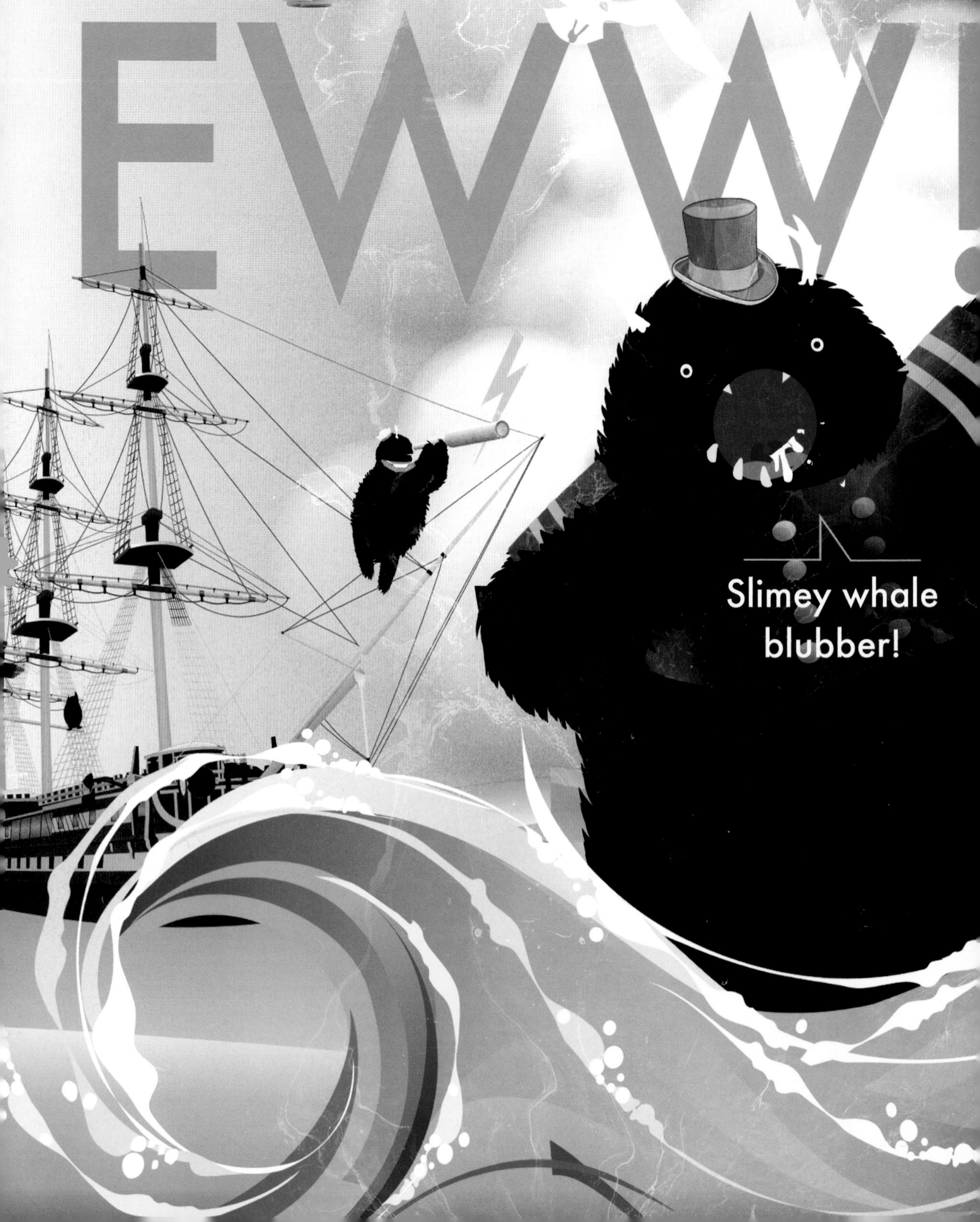
EWW!
Slimey whale
blubber!

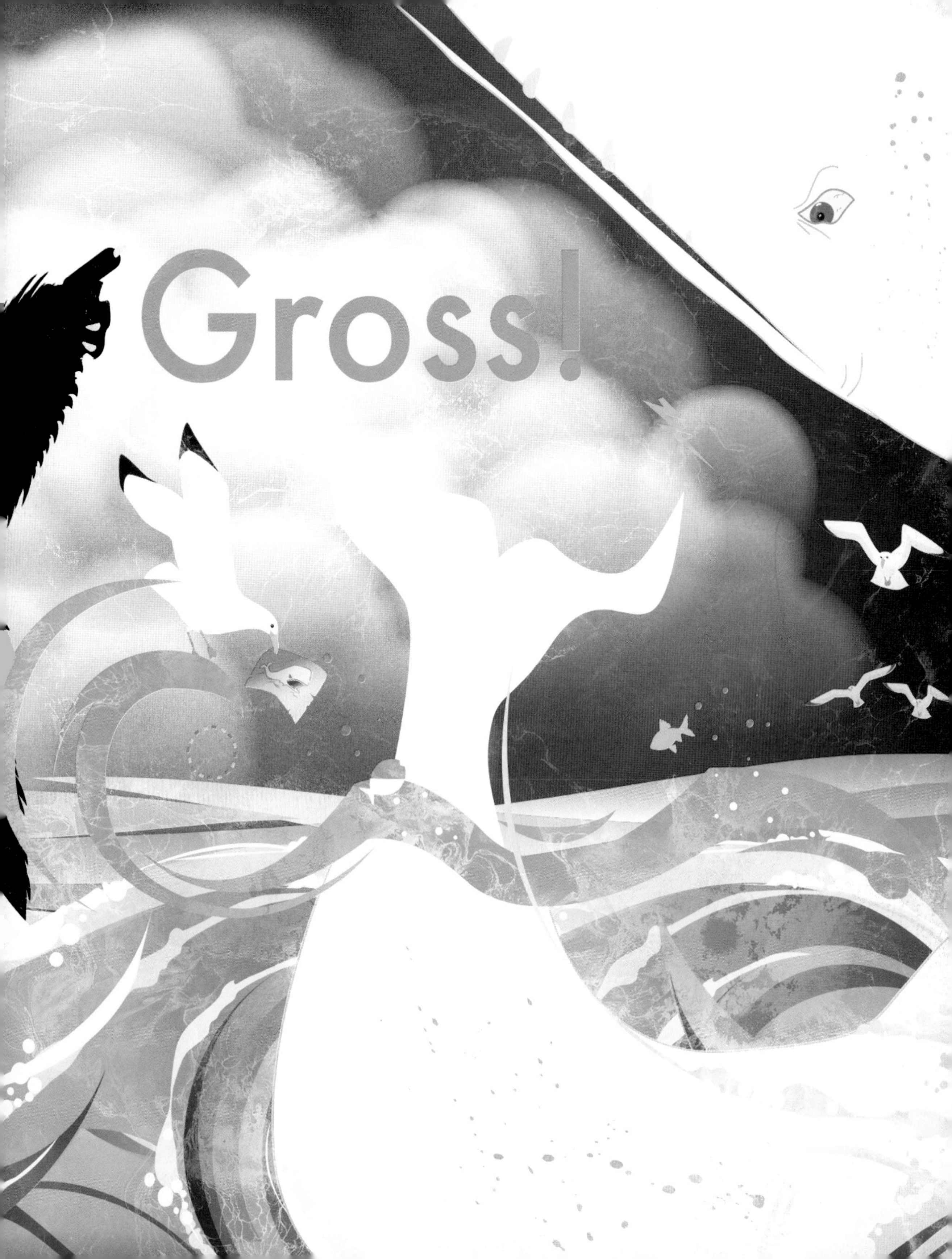
Gross!

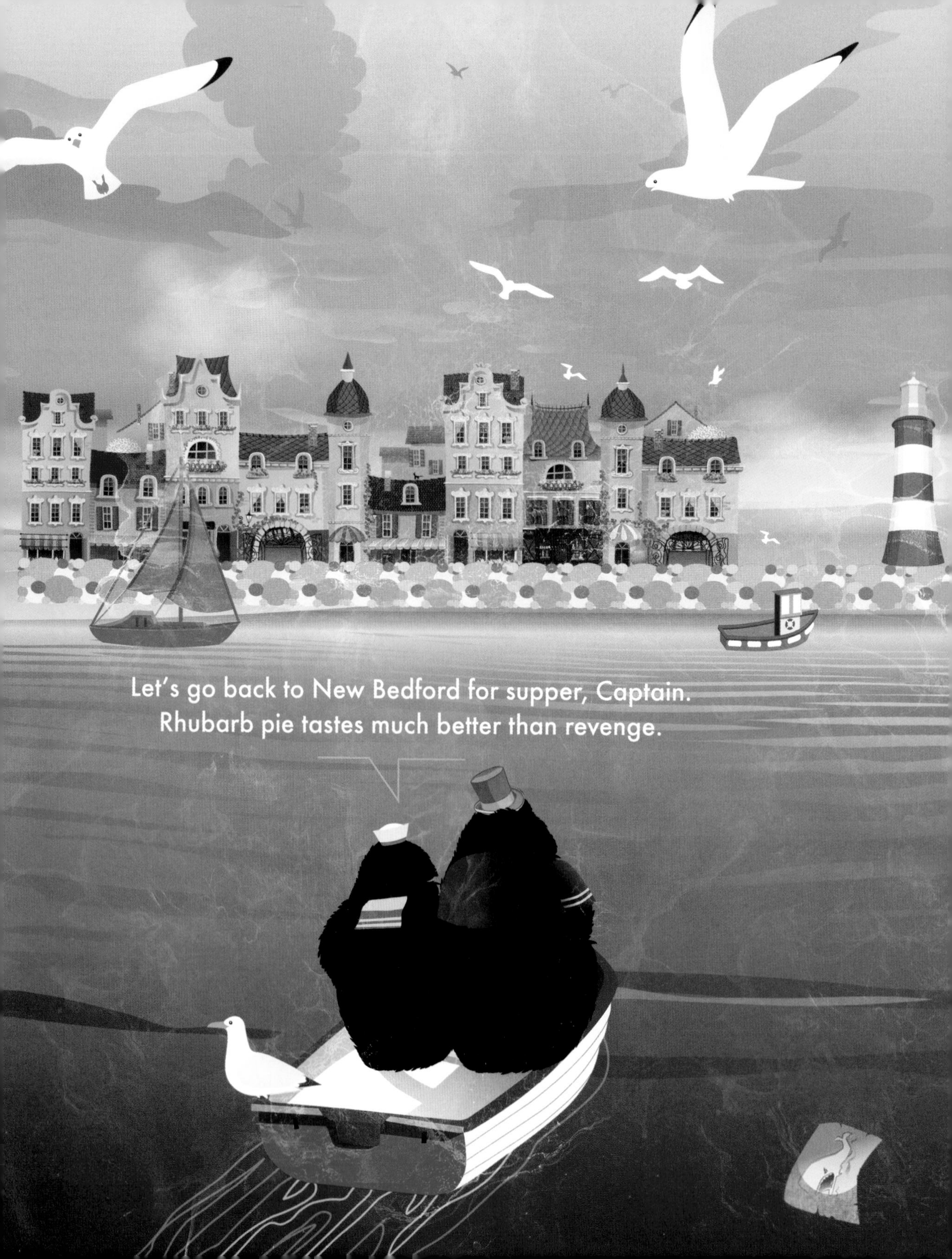
Let's go back to New Bedford for supper, Captain.
Rhubarb pie tastes much better than revenge.

The Tragedy of

HAMLET

Hamlet was very sleepy and wanted to say good night . . .

Something is yucky in the state of Denmark!

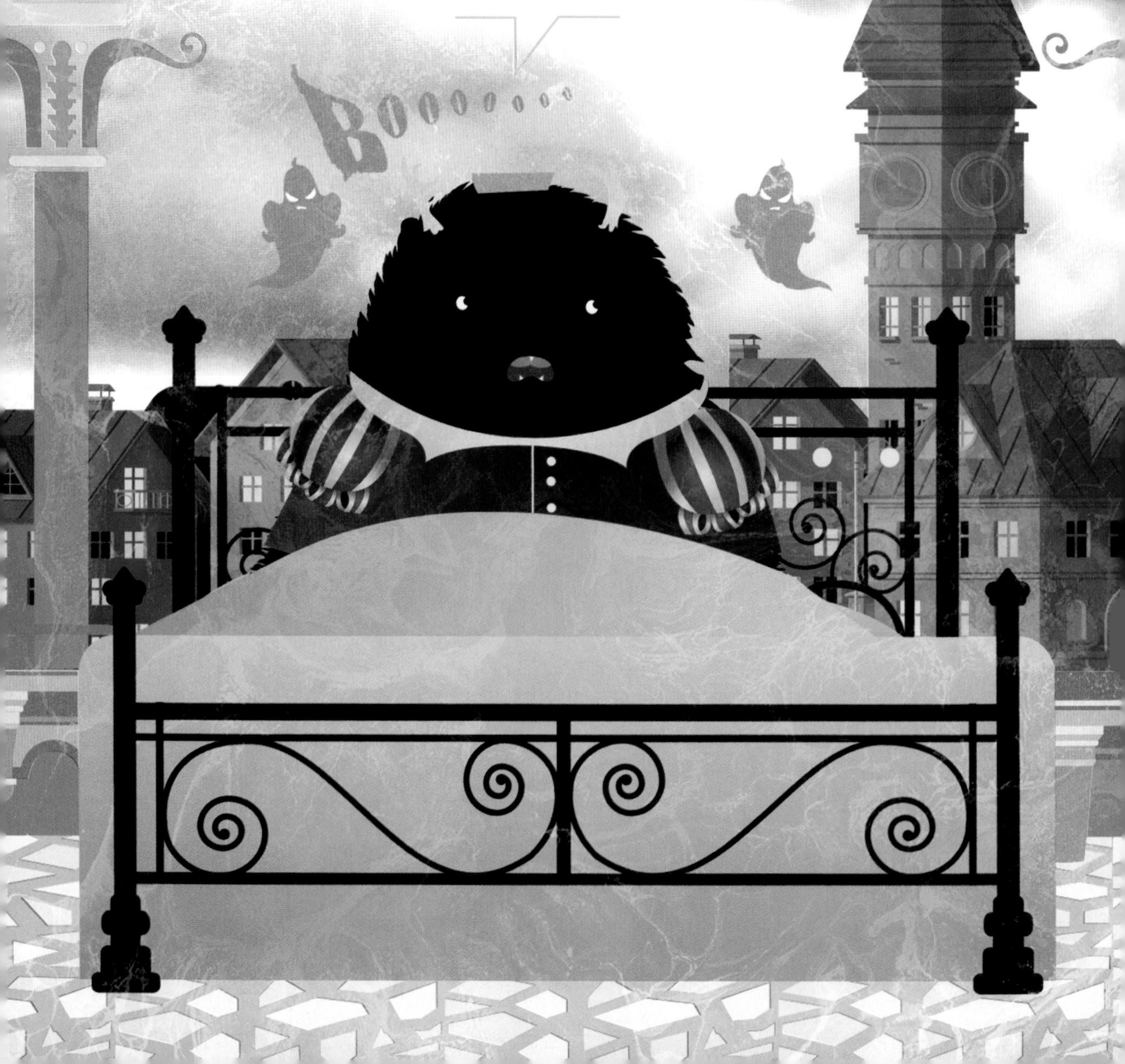

. . . but every time he tried to rest his head, a ghost made such a racket!

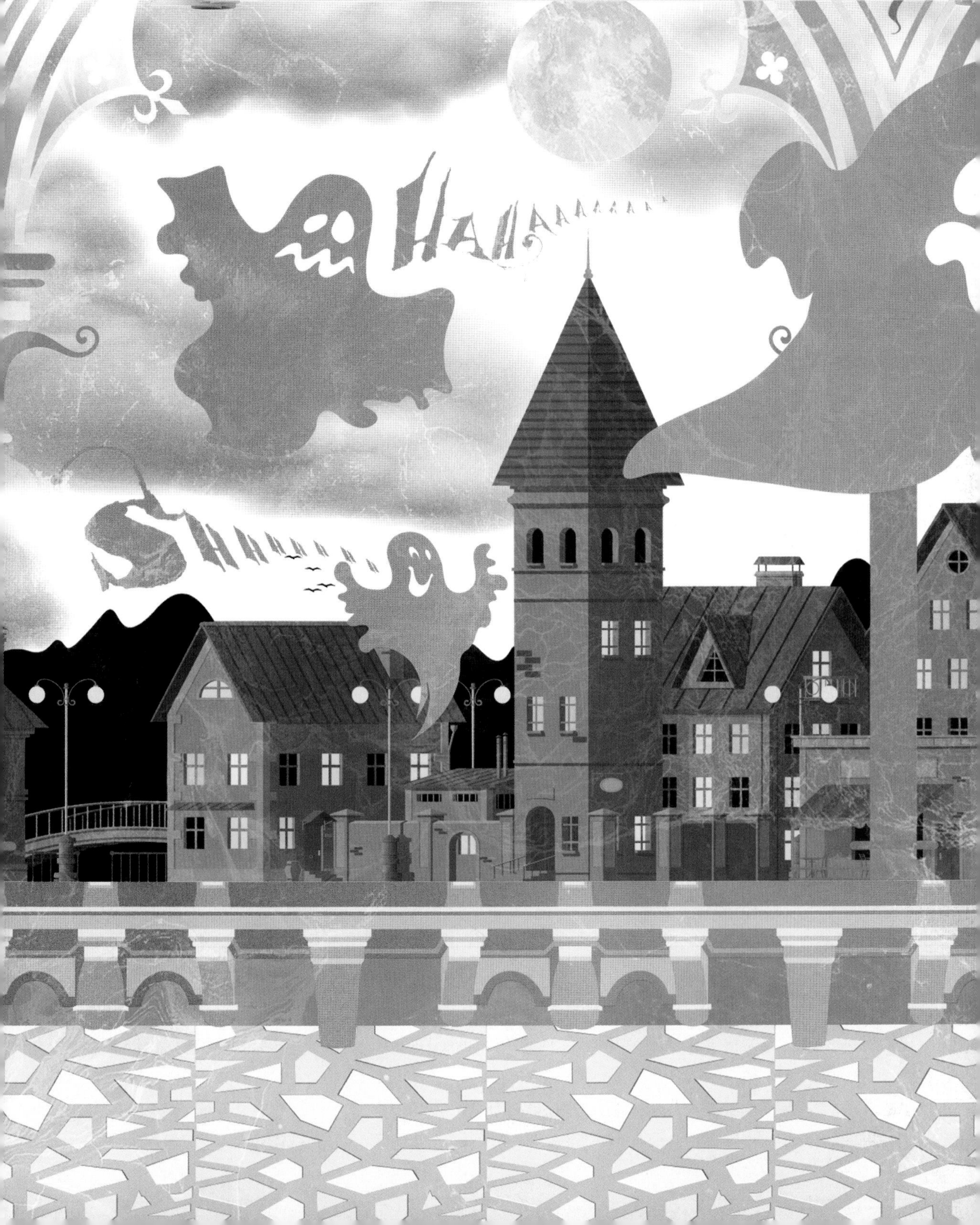

He tried sleeping everywhere–in the barnyard with the chickens,

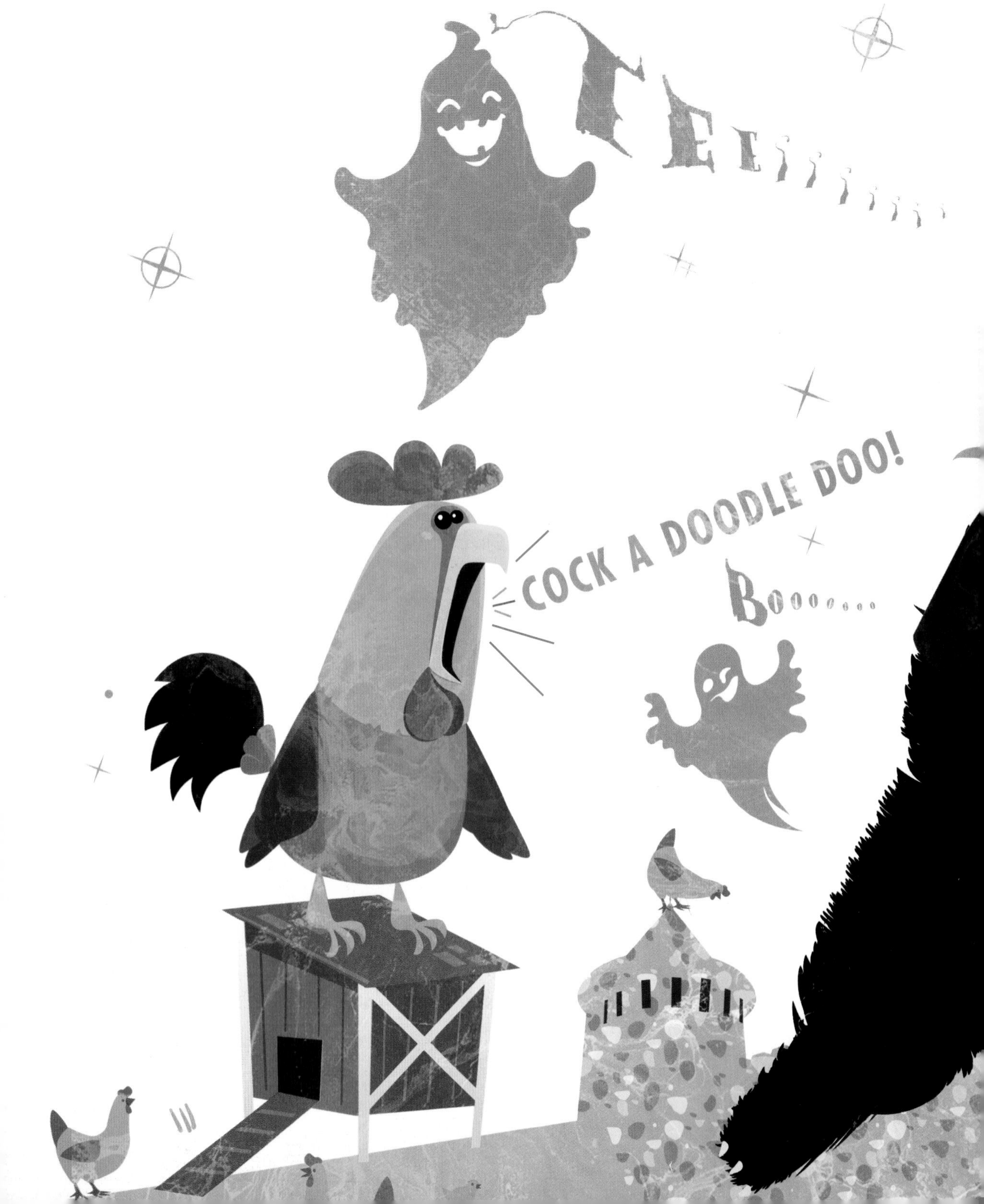

Teeeessssss
COCK A DOODLE DOO!
Boooooooo

on top of the castle wall,

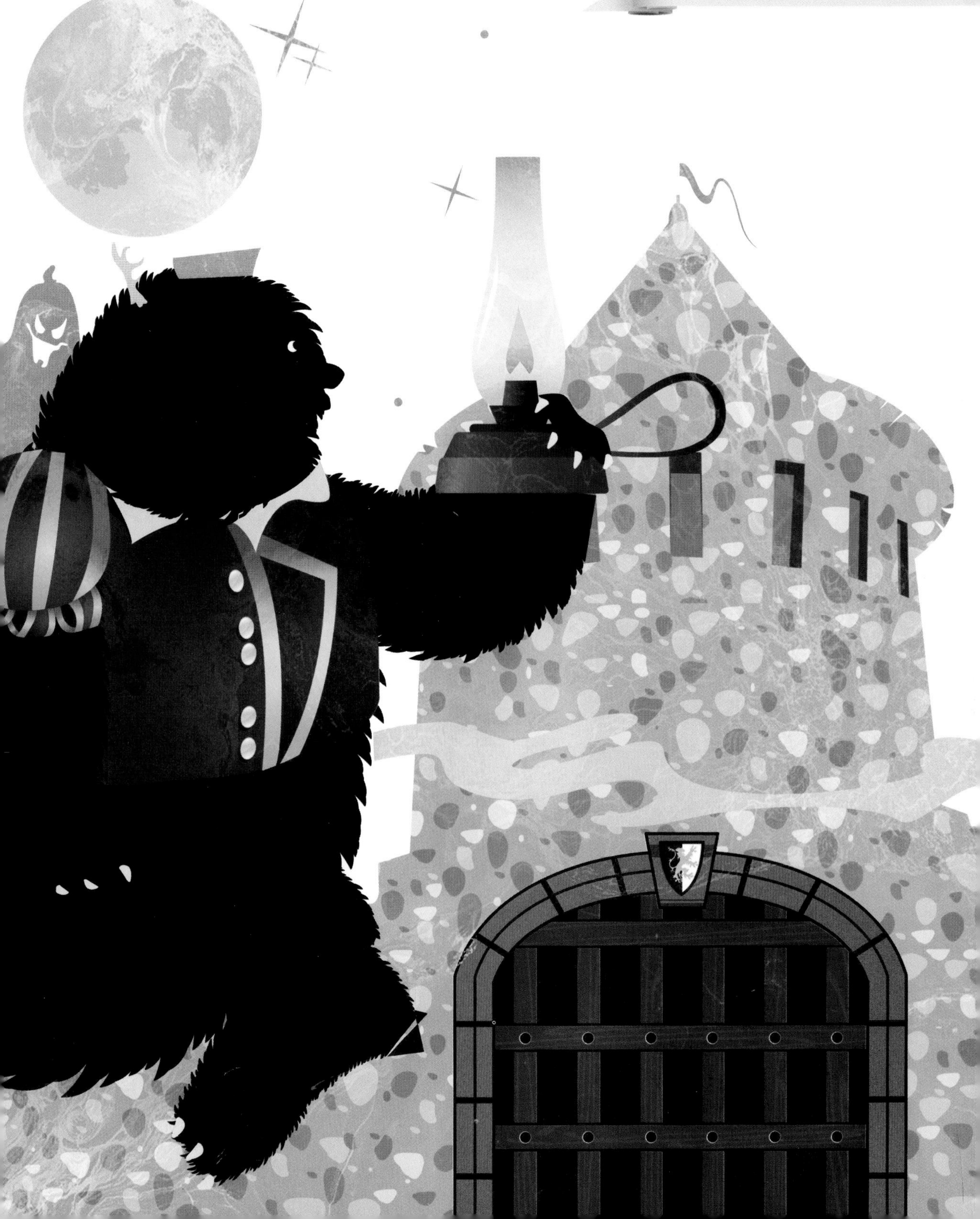

even in his mother's closet.

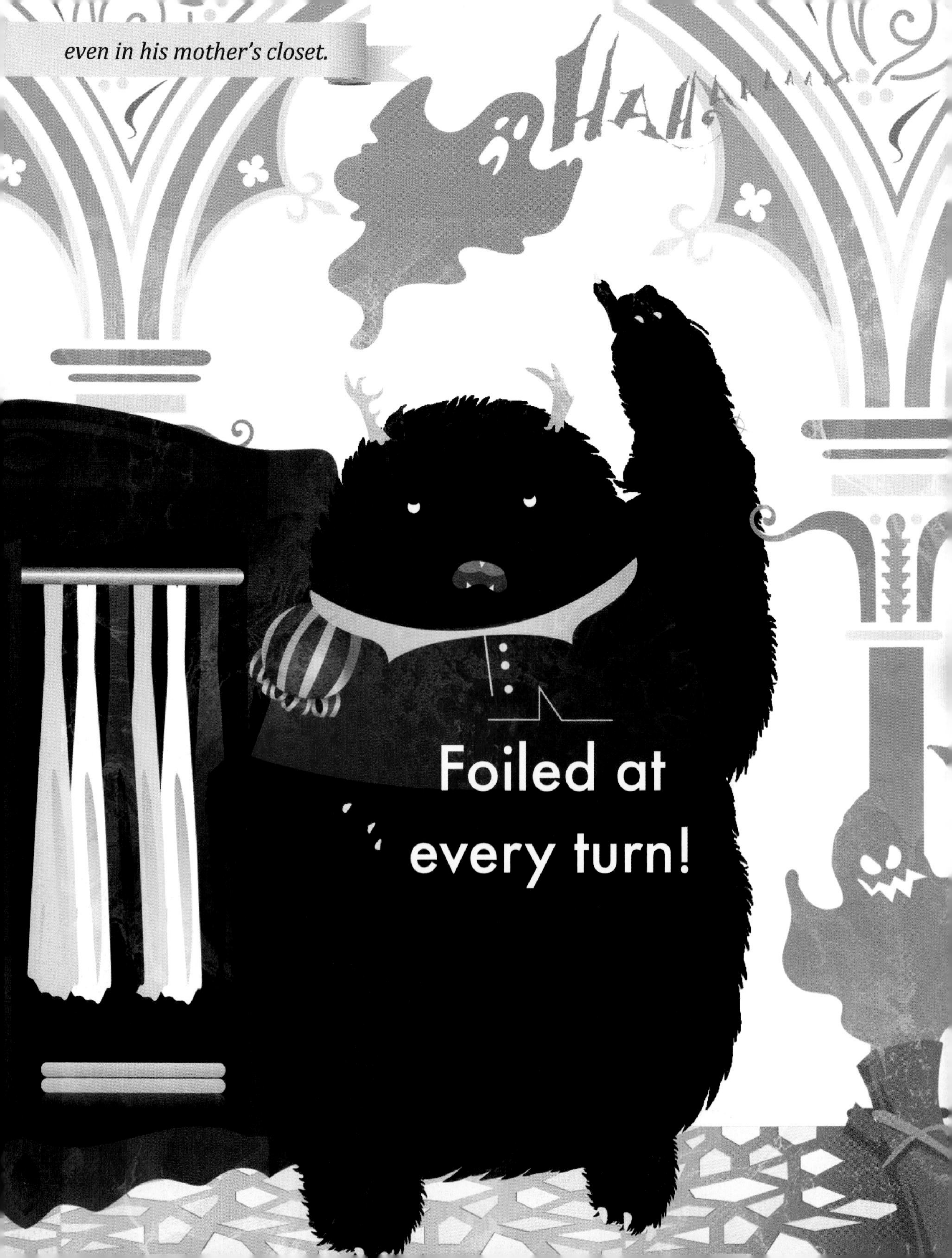
Foiled at
every turn!

Finally, Hamlet decided to talk some sense into that ghoul!

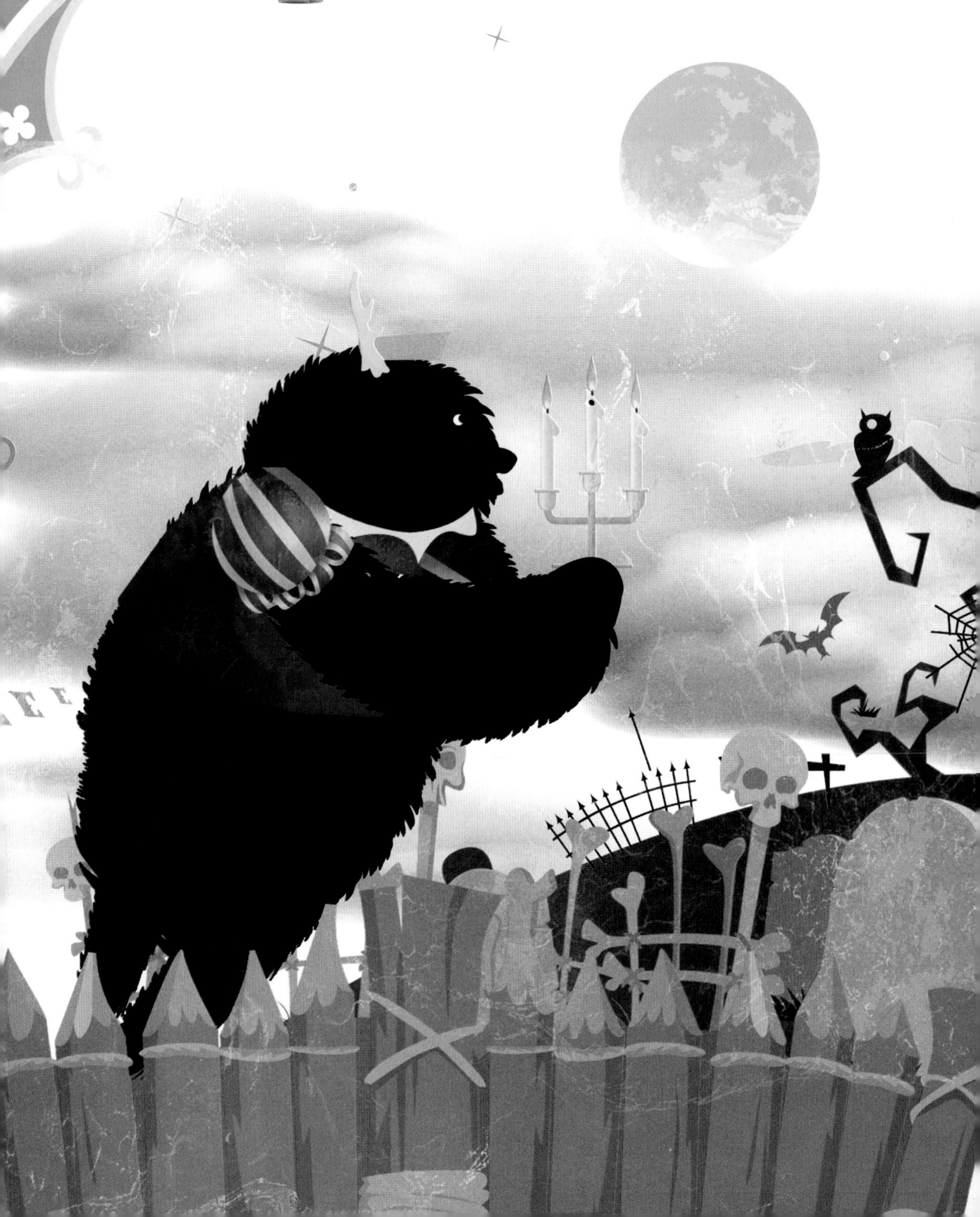

To be, or not

Look, ghost! To sleep,
maybe to dream—
I've had it up to here!

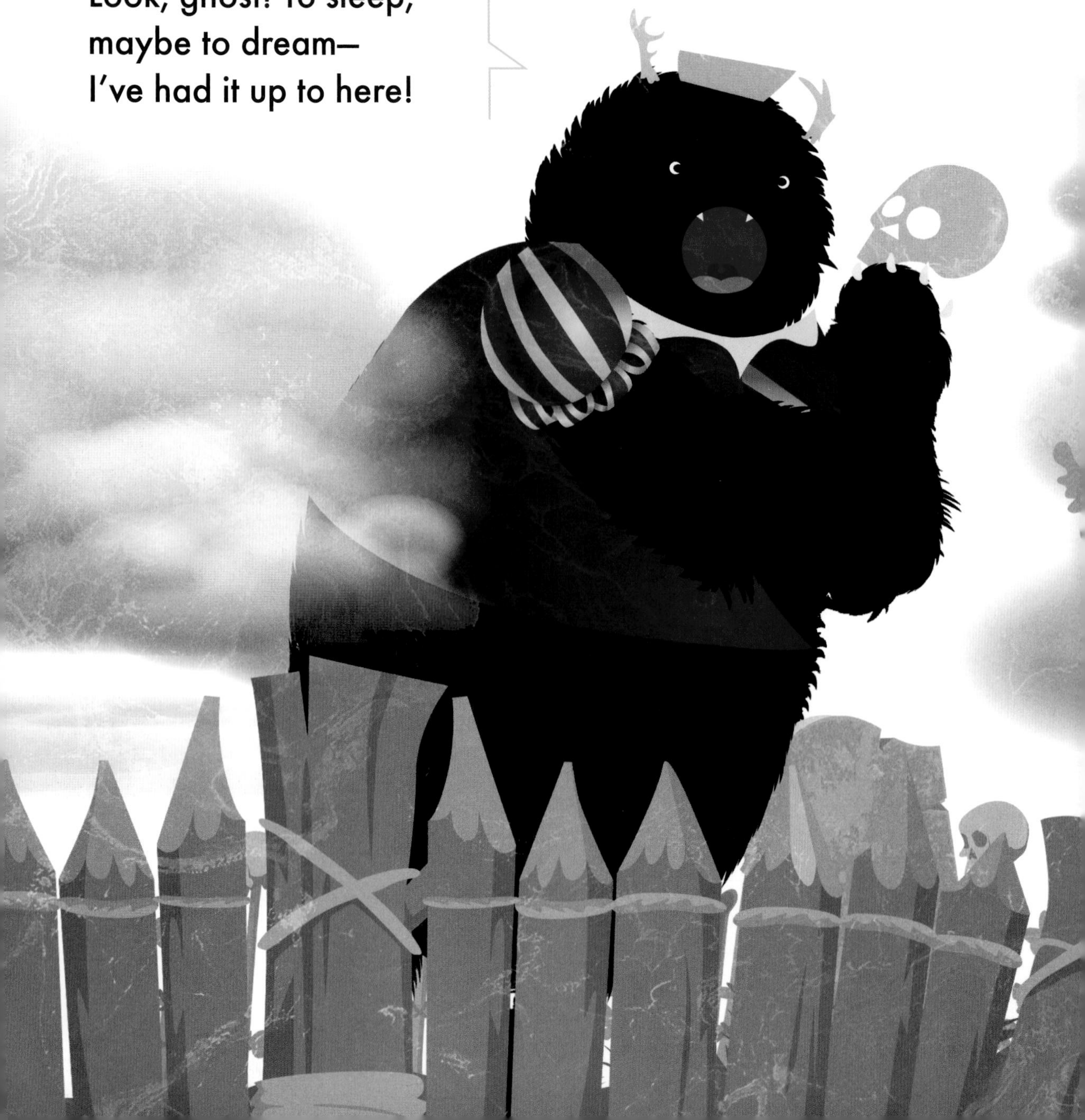

to be!

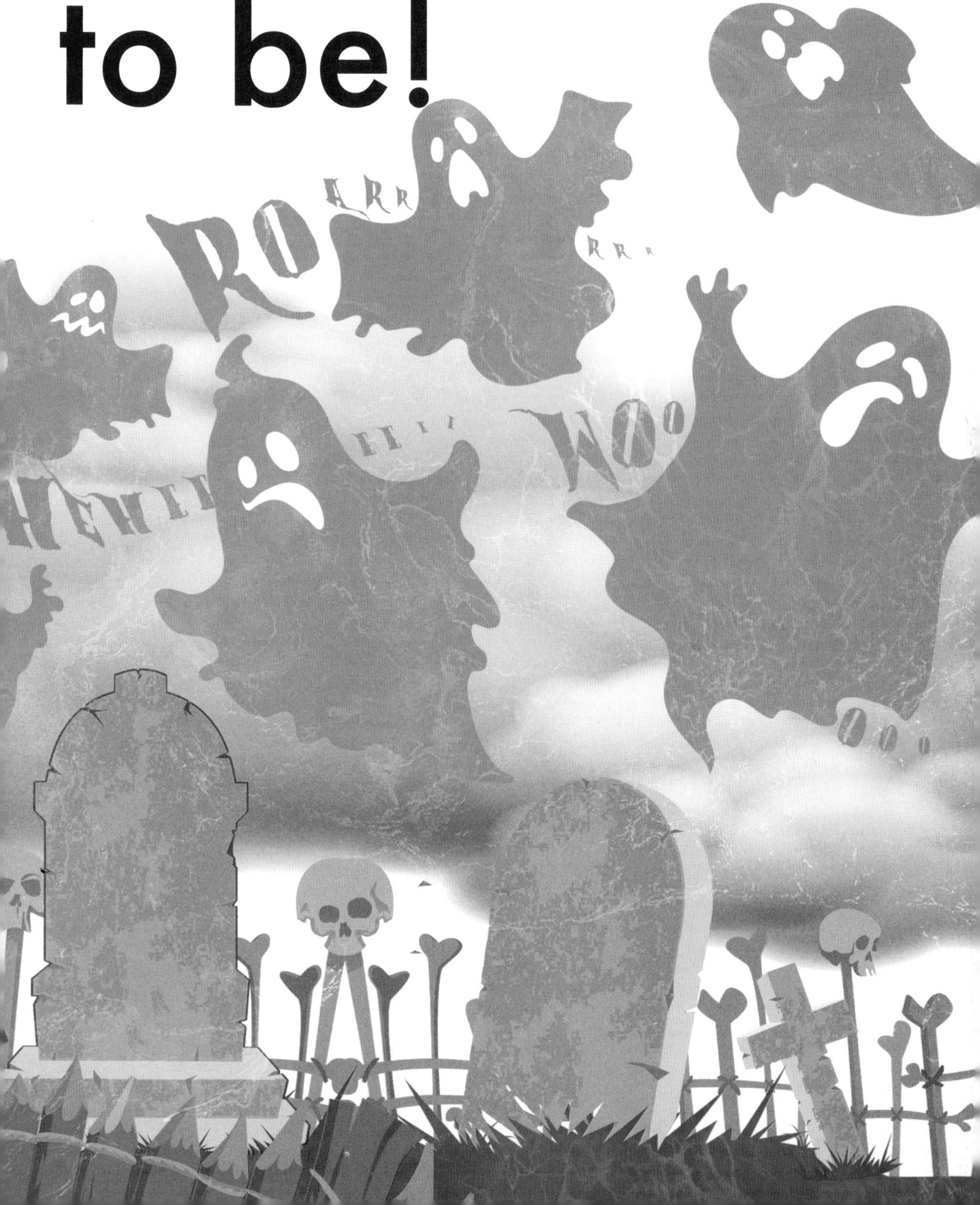
ROARRRRR
HEHEEEE
WOOOOO

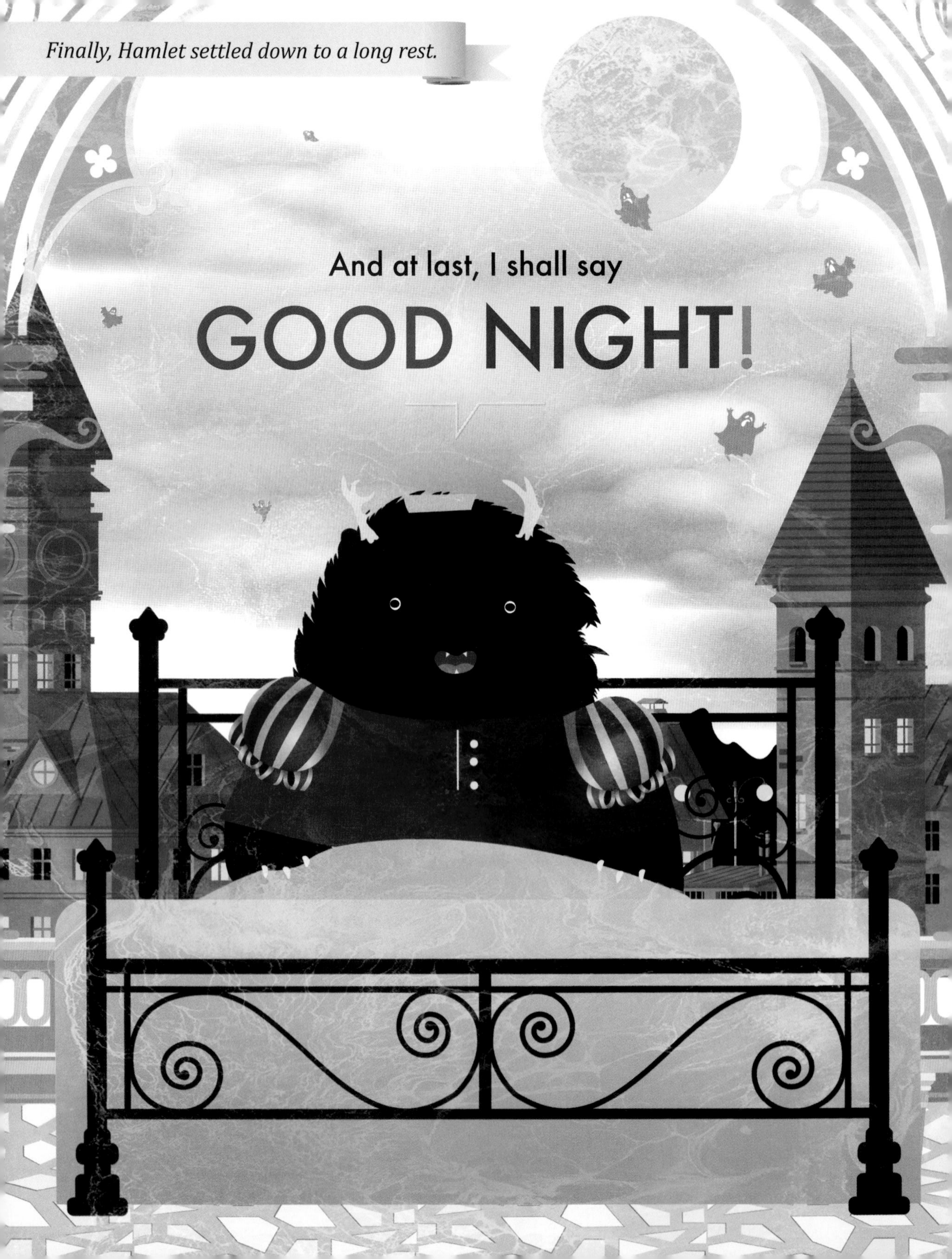
Finally, Hamlet settled down to a long rest.
And at last, I shall say
GOOD NIGHT!

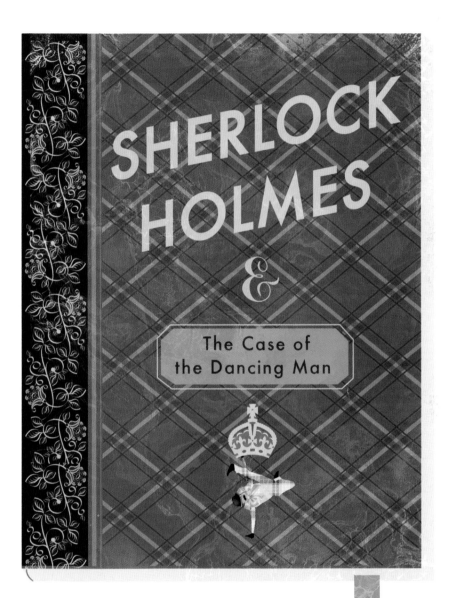

SHERLOCK HOLMES

&

The Case of
the Dancing Man

When a crime rocked Scotland Yard, Sherlock Holmes was on the case . . .

Quick, Watson, quick!

The Dancing Man has stolen the Crown Jewels!

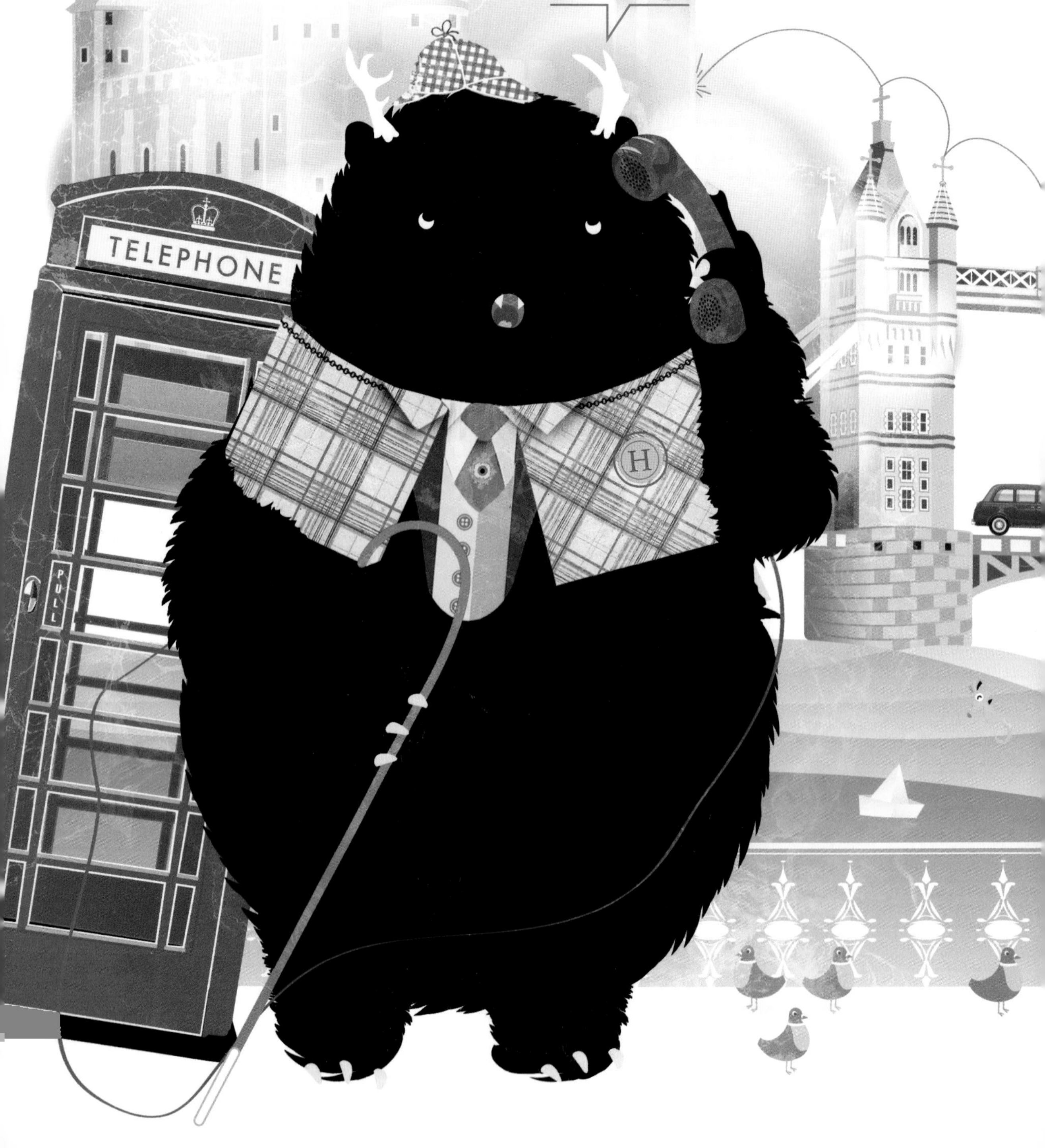
TELEPHONE
PULL
H

. . . along with his partner, Dr. Watson.

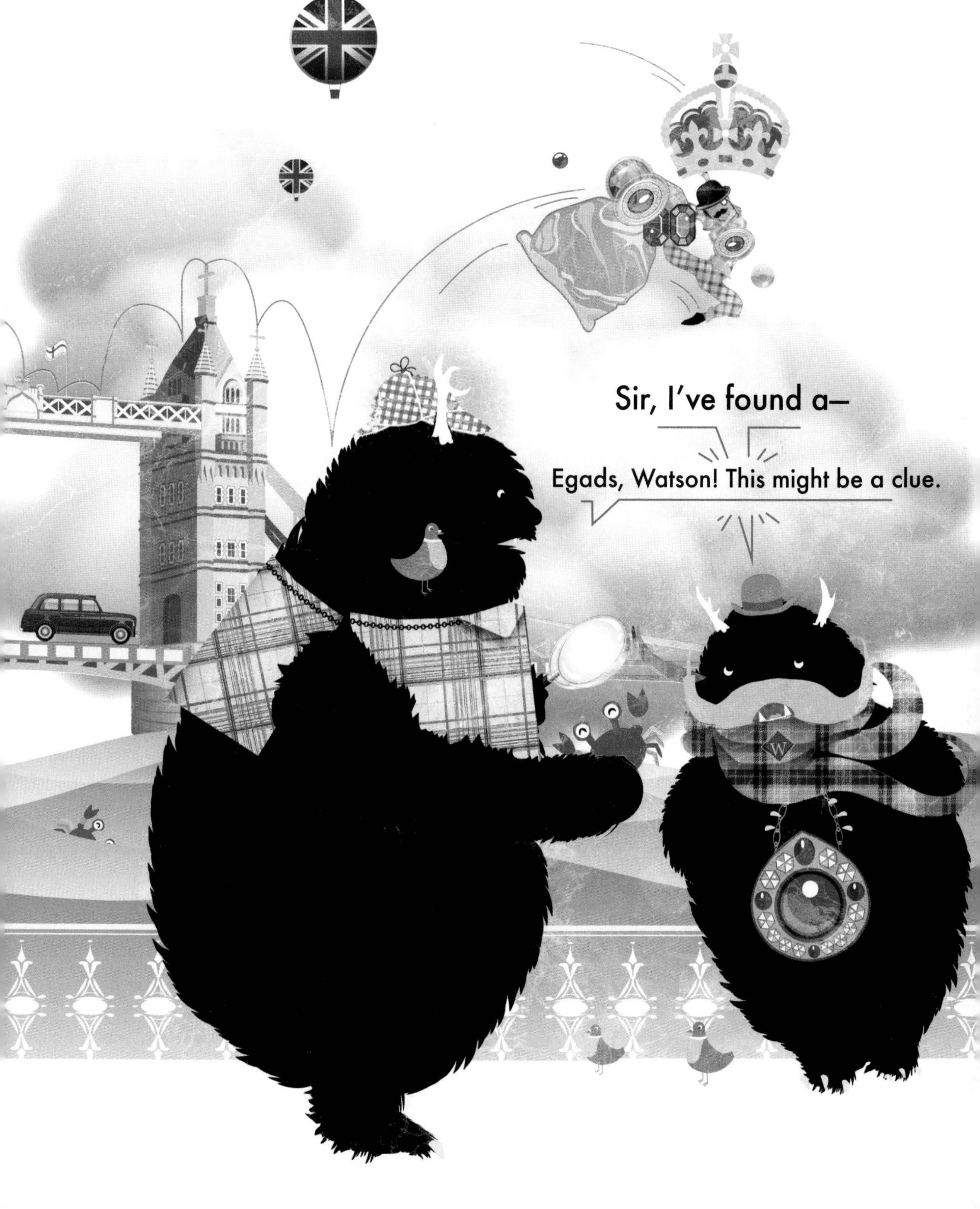
Sir, I've found a—
Egads, Watson! This might be a clue.

Watson spied the crook!

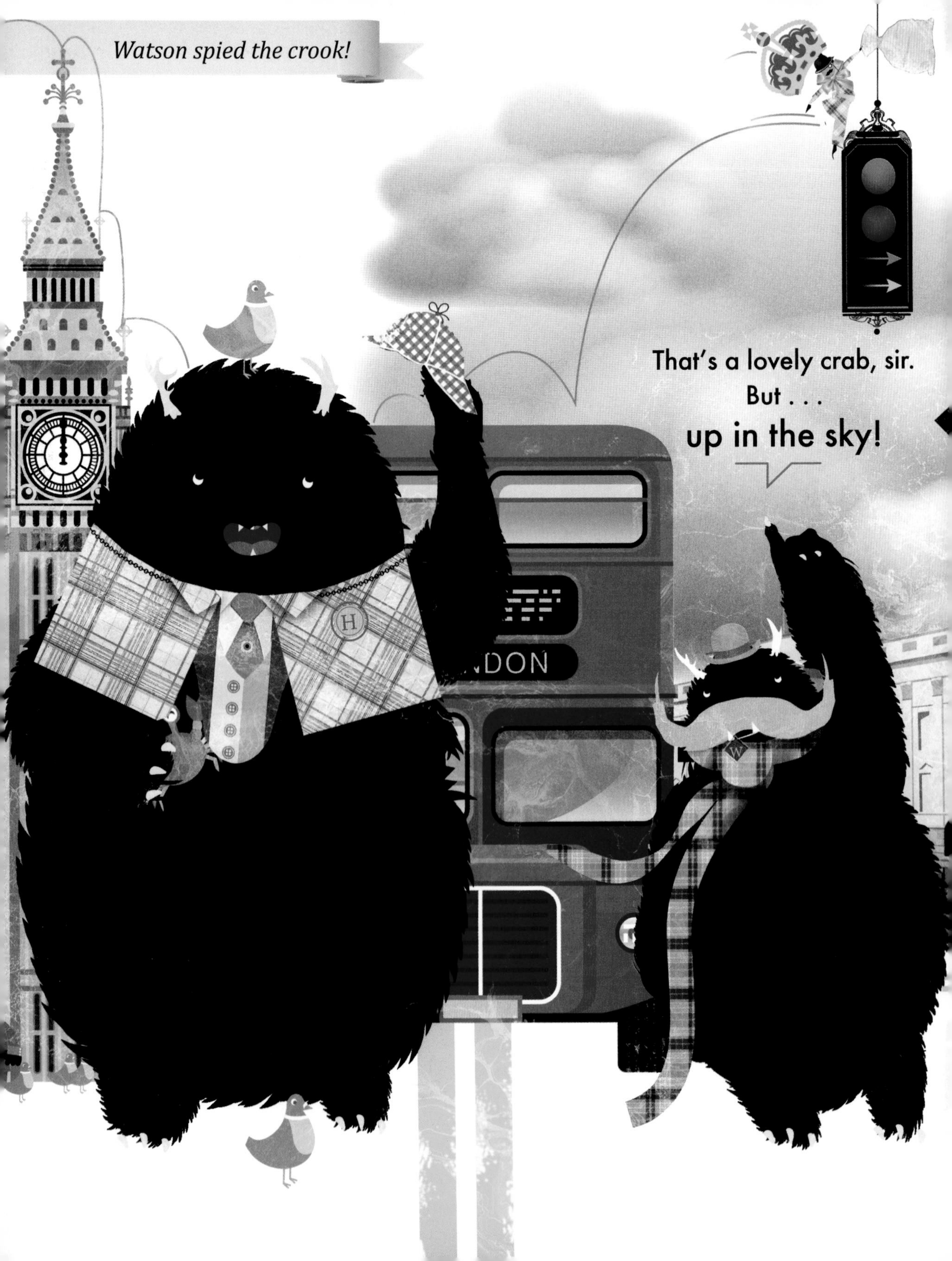
That's a lovely crab, sir.
But . . .
up in the sky!

He heroically chased the man through London, while Holmes remained unaware.

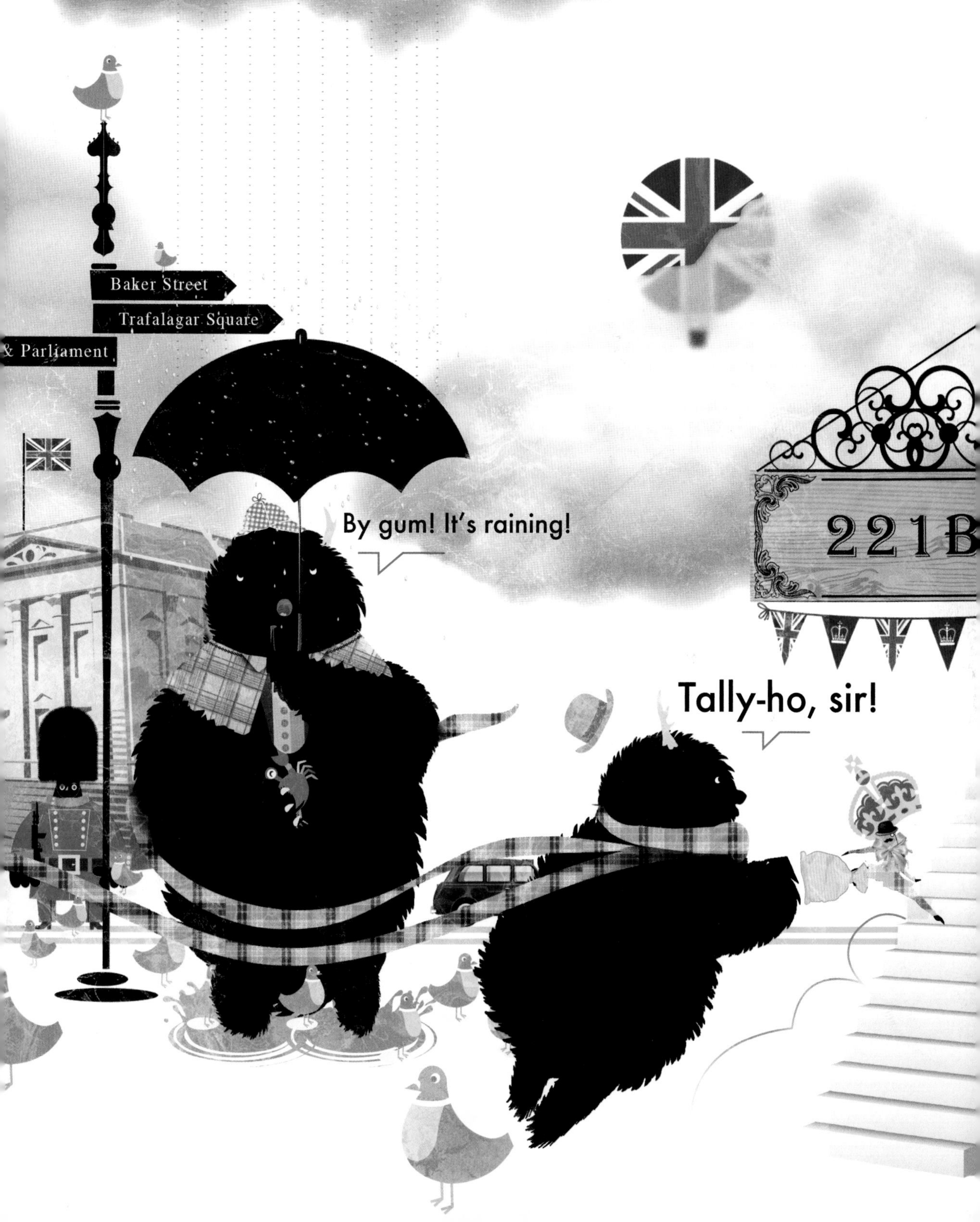
Baker Street
Trafalagar Square
& Parliament
By gum! It's raining!
221B
Tally-ho, sir!

Holmes bumbled along, while Watson was hot on the trail!

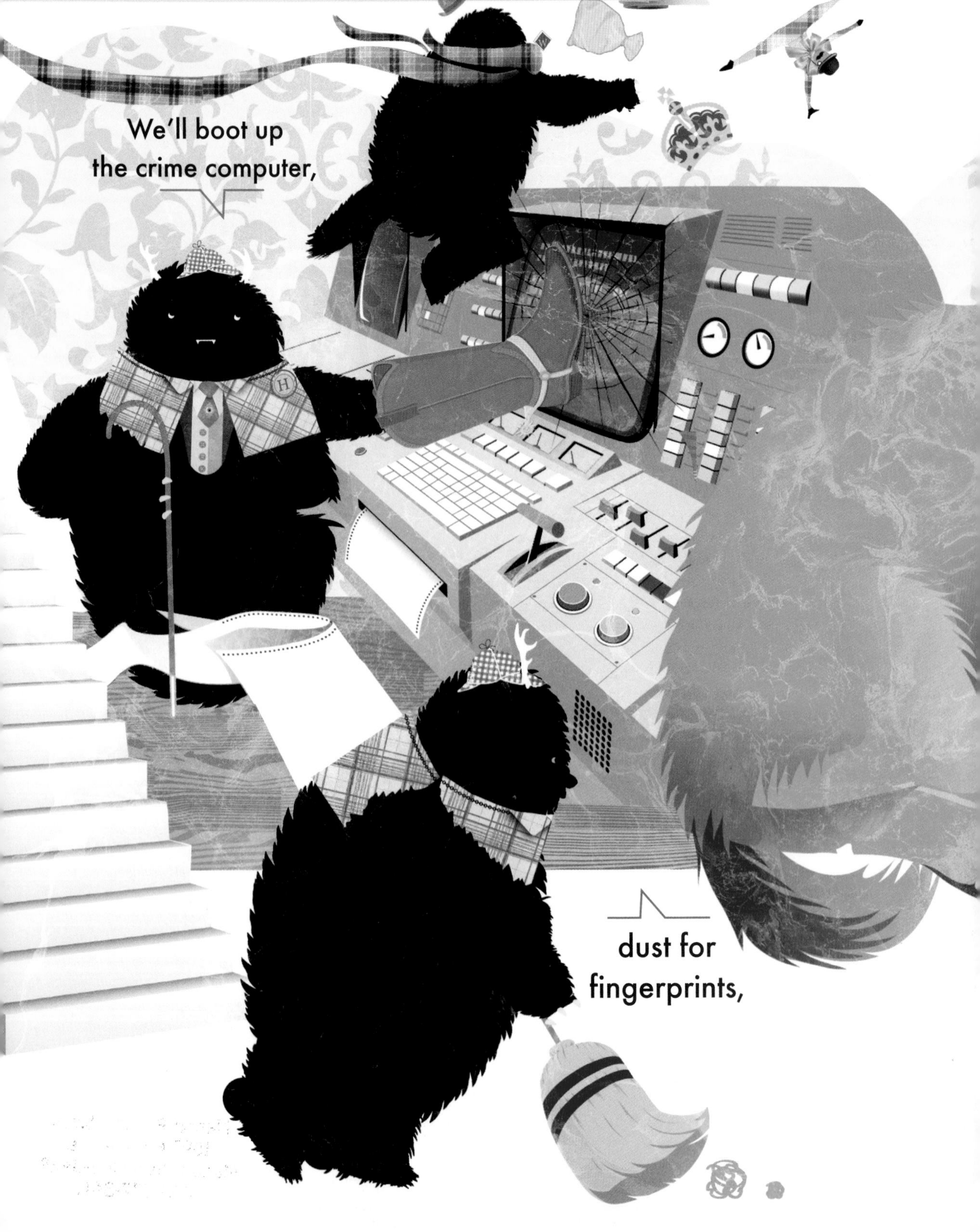
We'll boot up the crime computer,
dust for fingerprints,

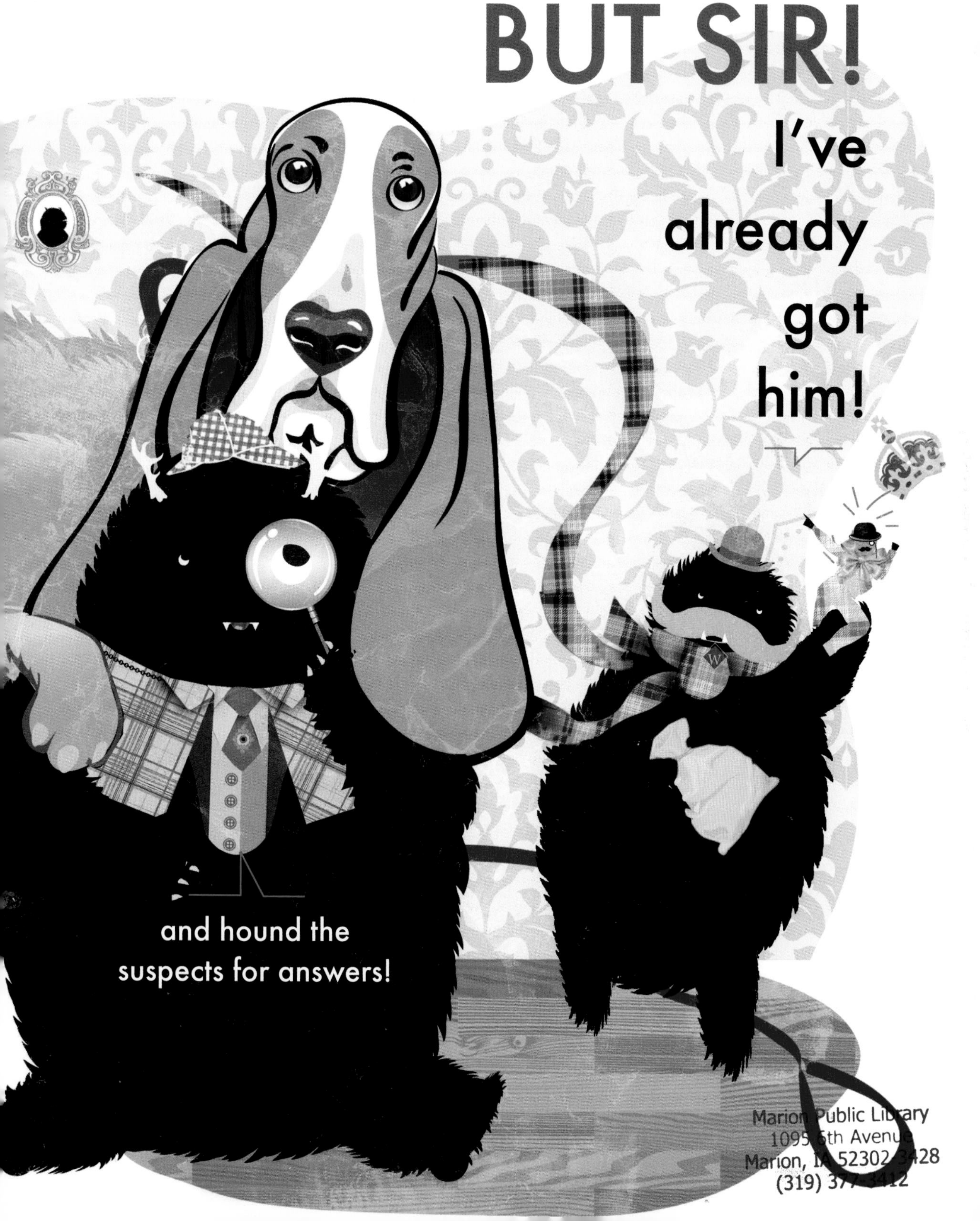
BUT SIR! I've already got him!
and hound the suspects for answers!

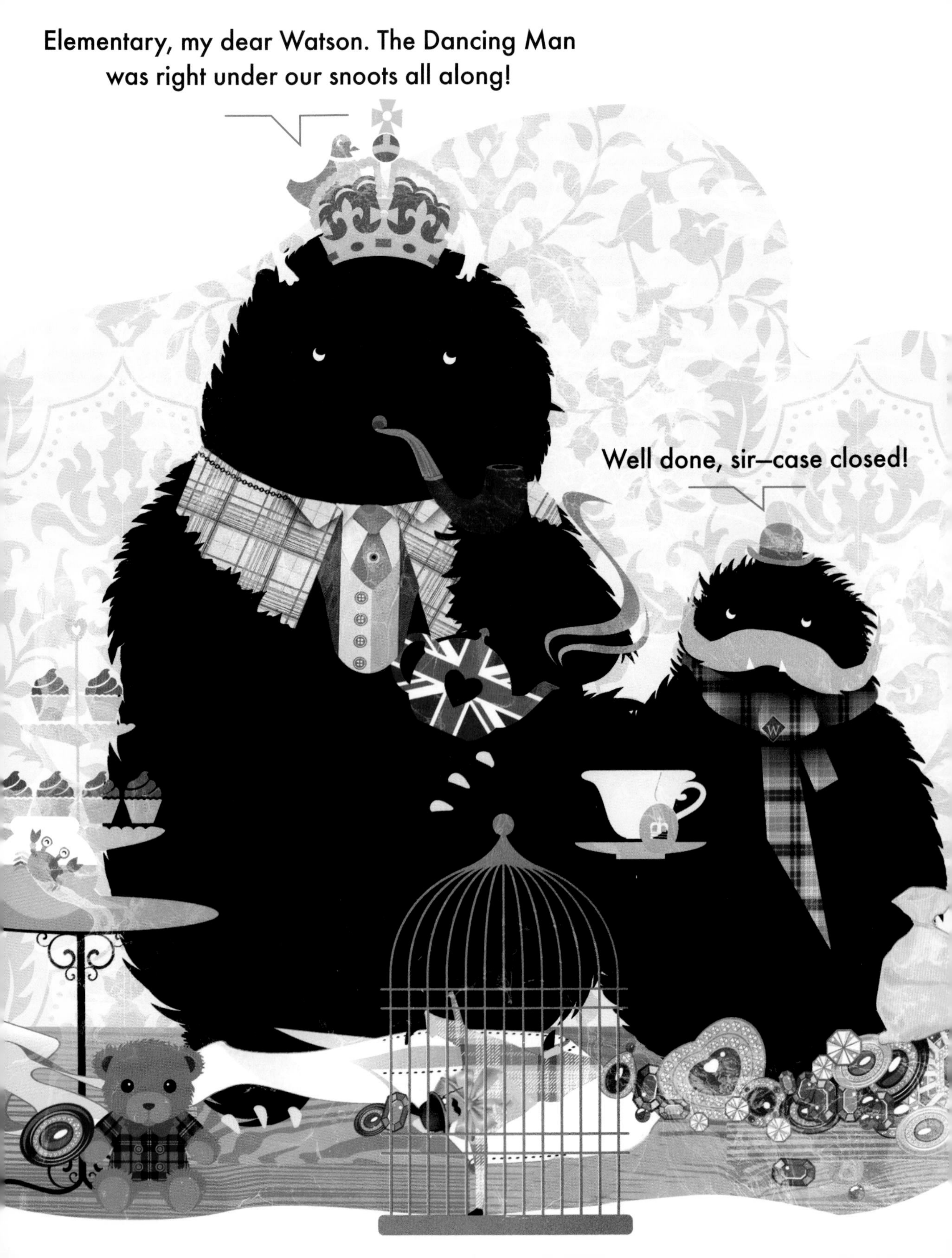
Elementary, my dear Watson. The Dancing Man was right under our snoots all along!
Well done, sir—case closed!

PRIDE
&
PREJUDICE

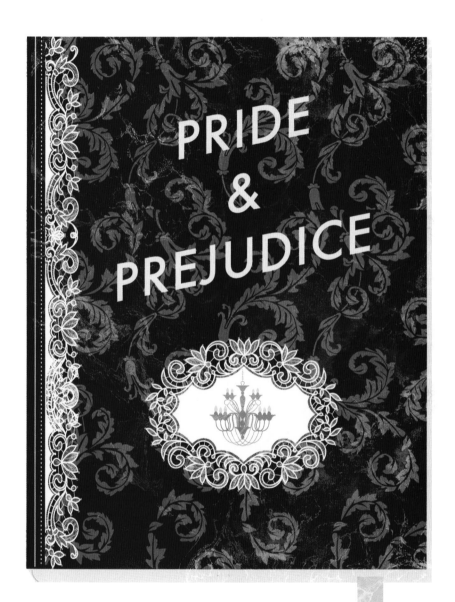

At a gilded gala in the good town of Hertfordshire,

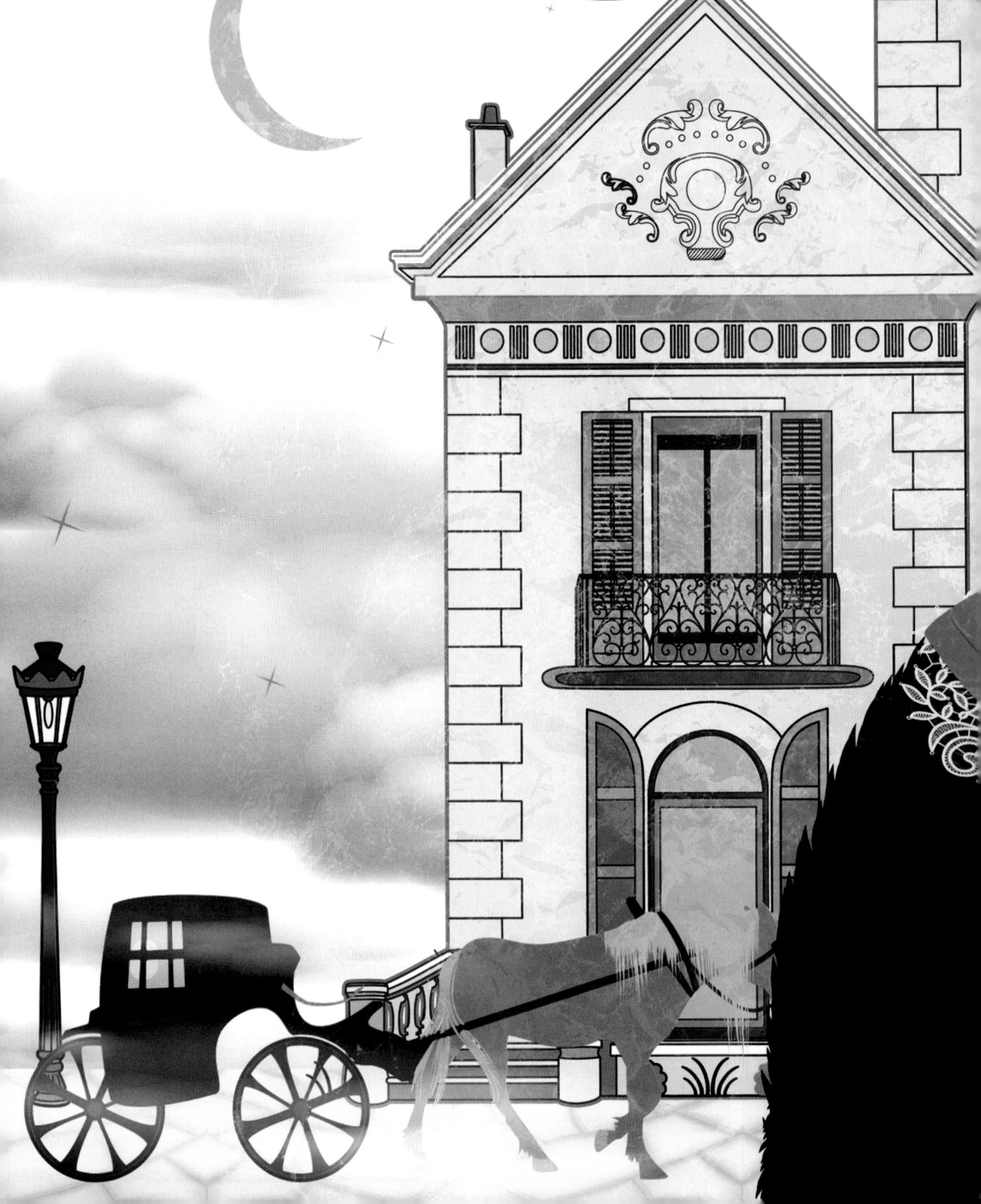

the young Elizabeth asked Mr. Darcy to dance.

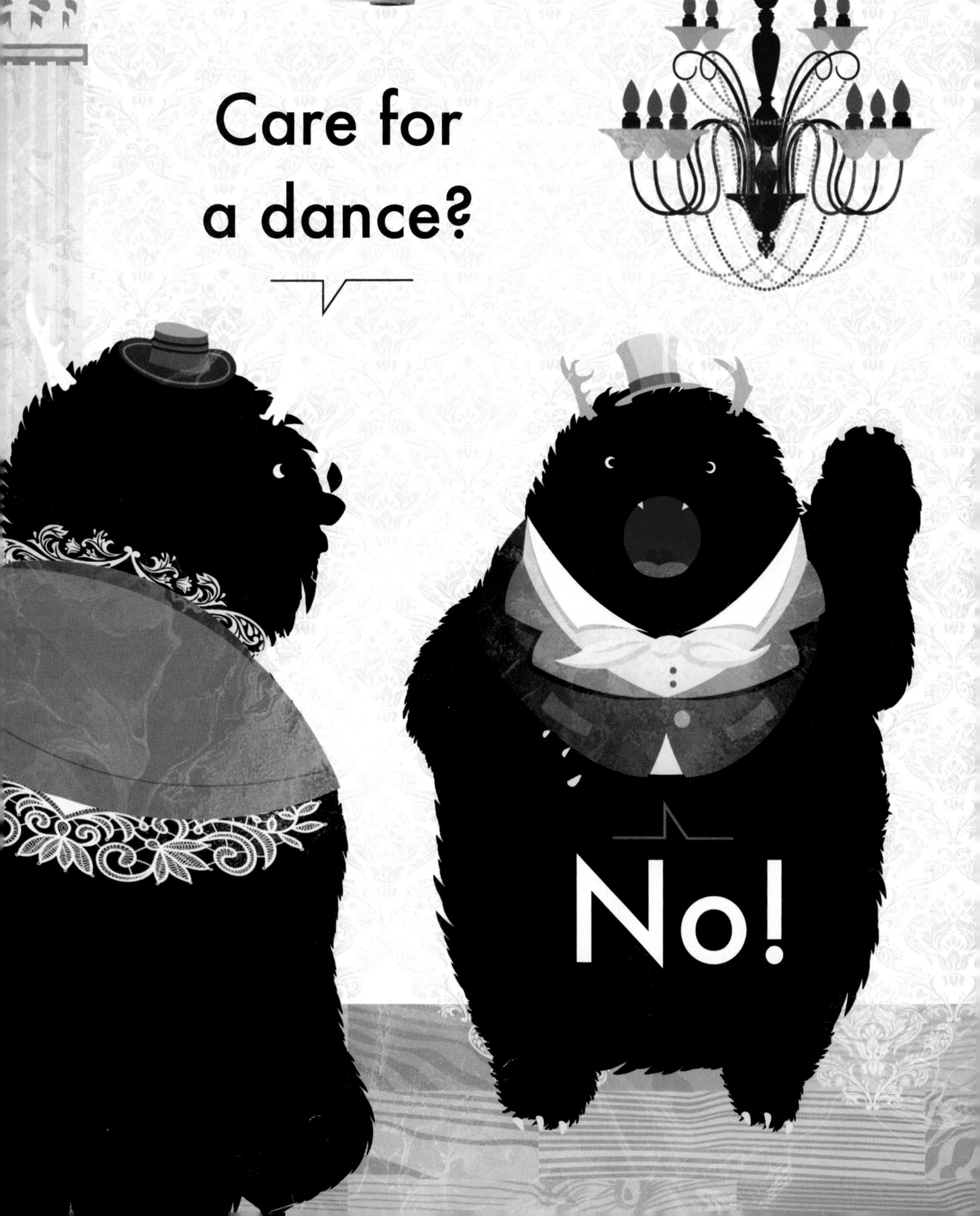
Care for a dance?
No!

Later on, after careful reconsidering, Mr. Darcy asked Elizabeth to dance.

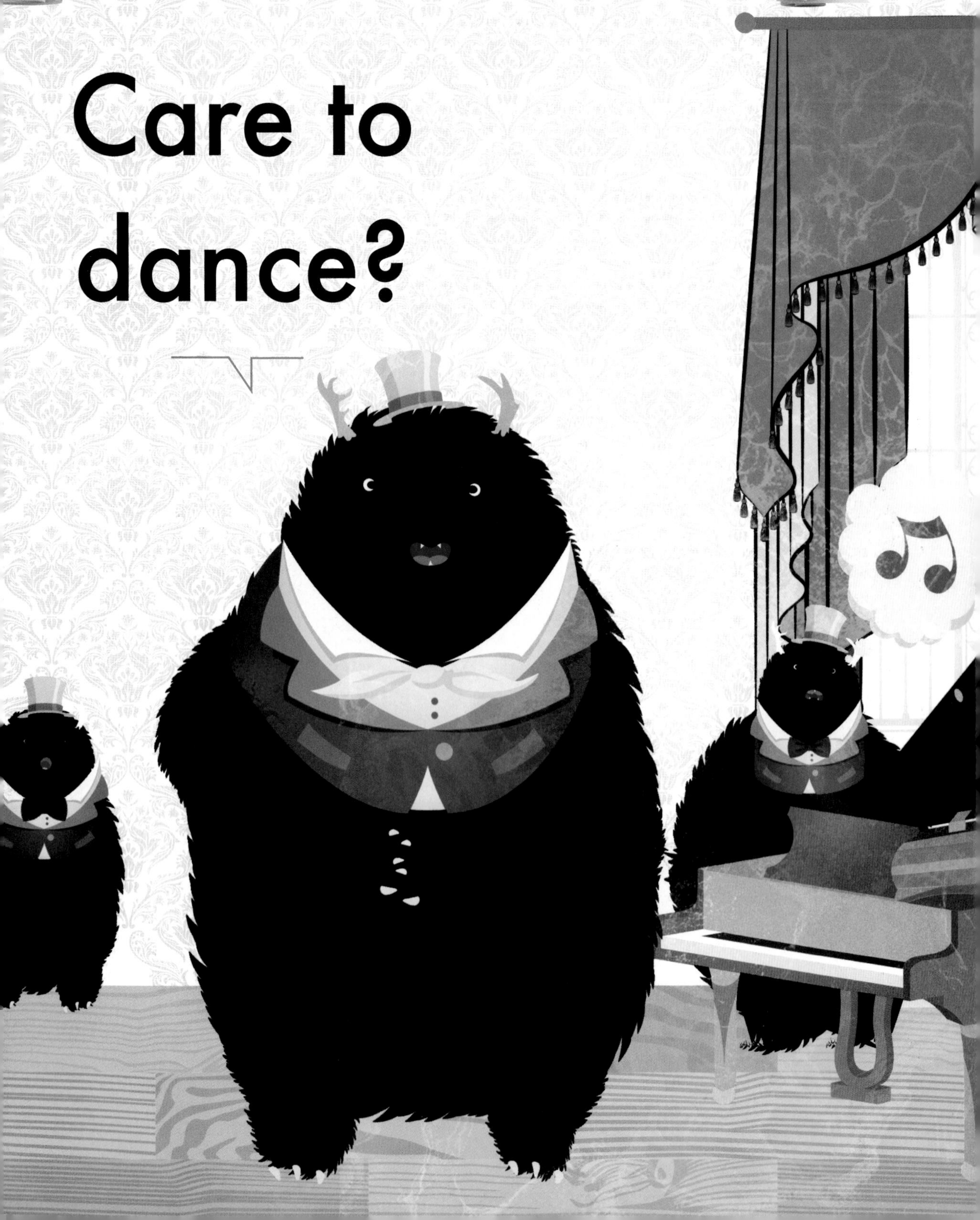
Care to dance?

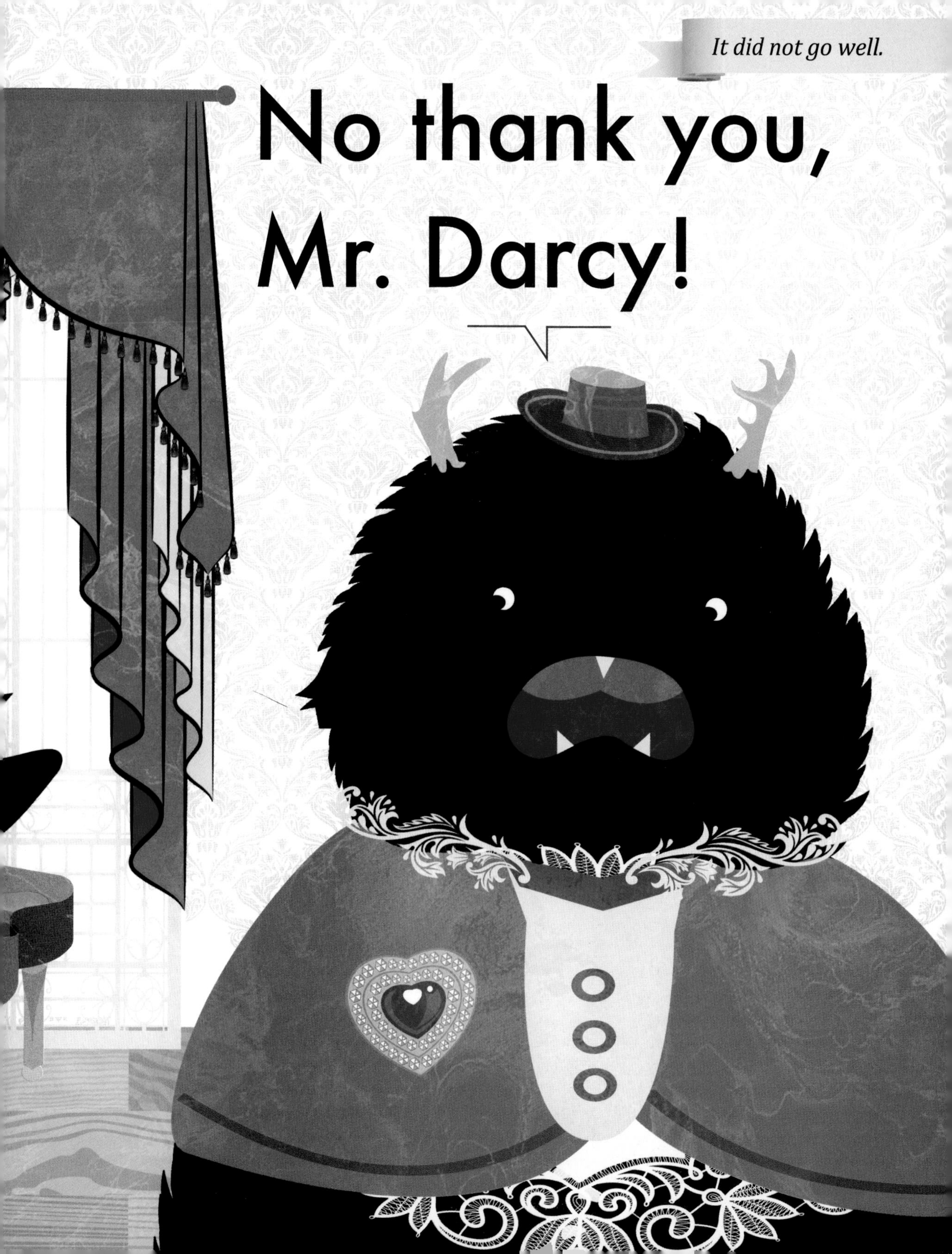
It did not go well.
No thank you, Mr. Darcy!

They watched the other couples dance:
the grand march, the waltz—what fun!

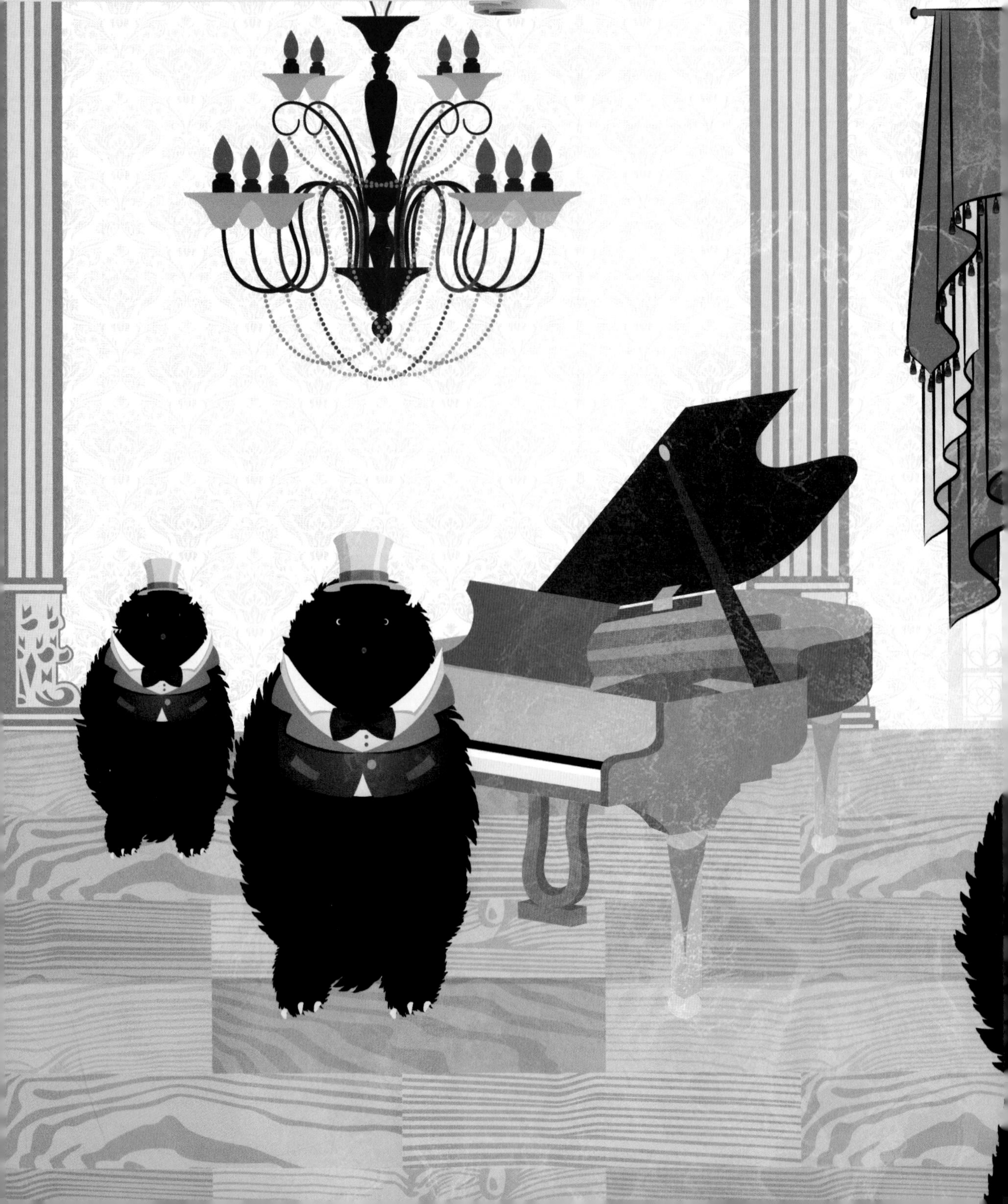

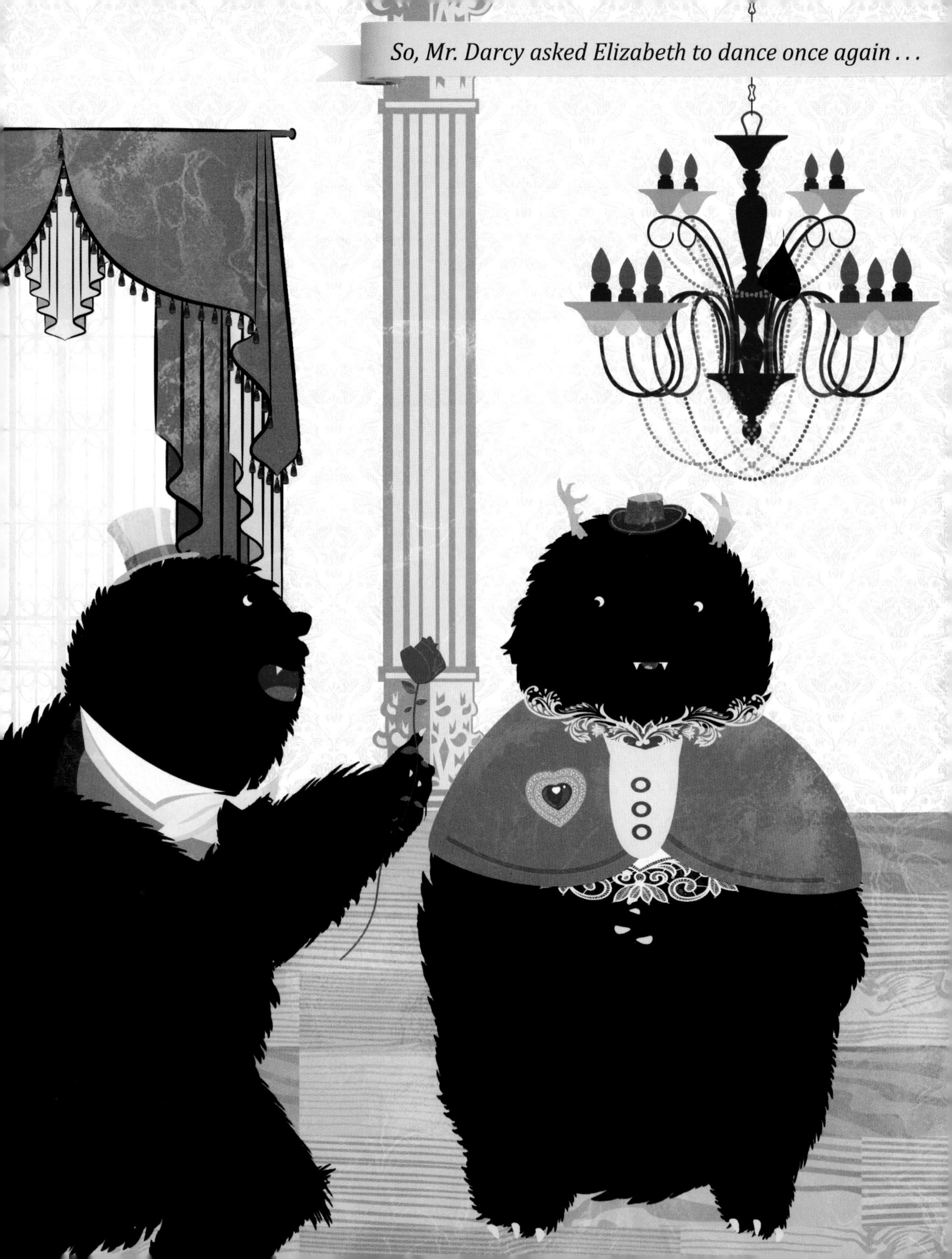
So, Mr. Darcy asked Elizabeth to dance once again . . .

and at last, they found their happy ending.

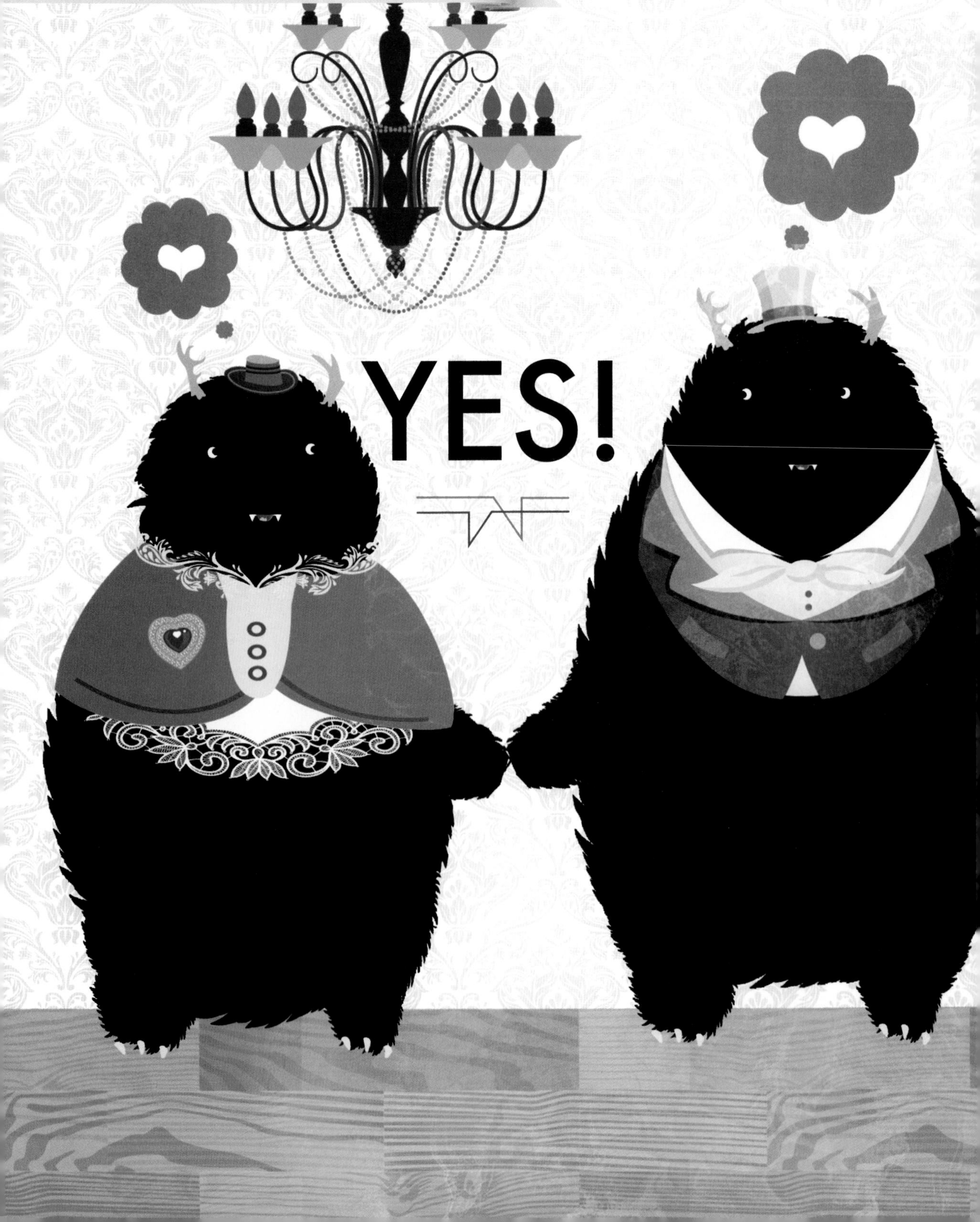
YES!

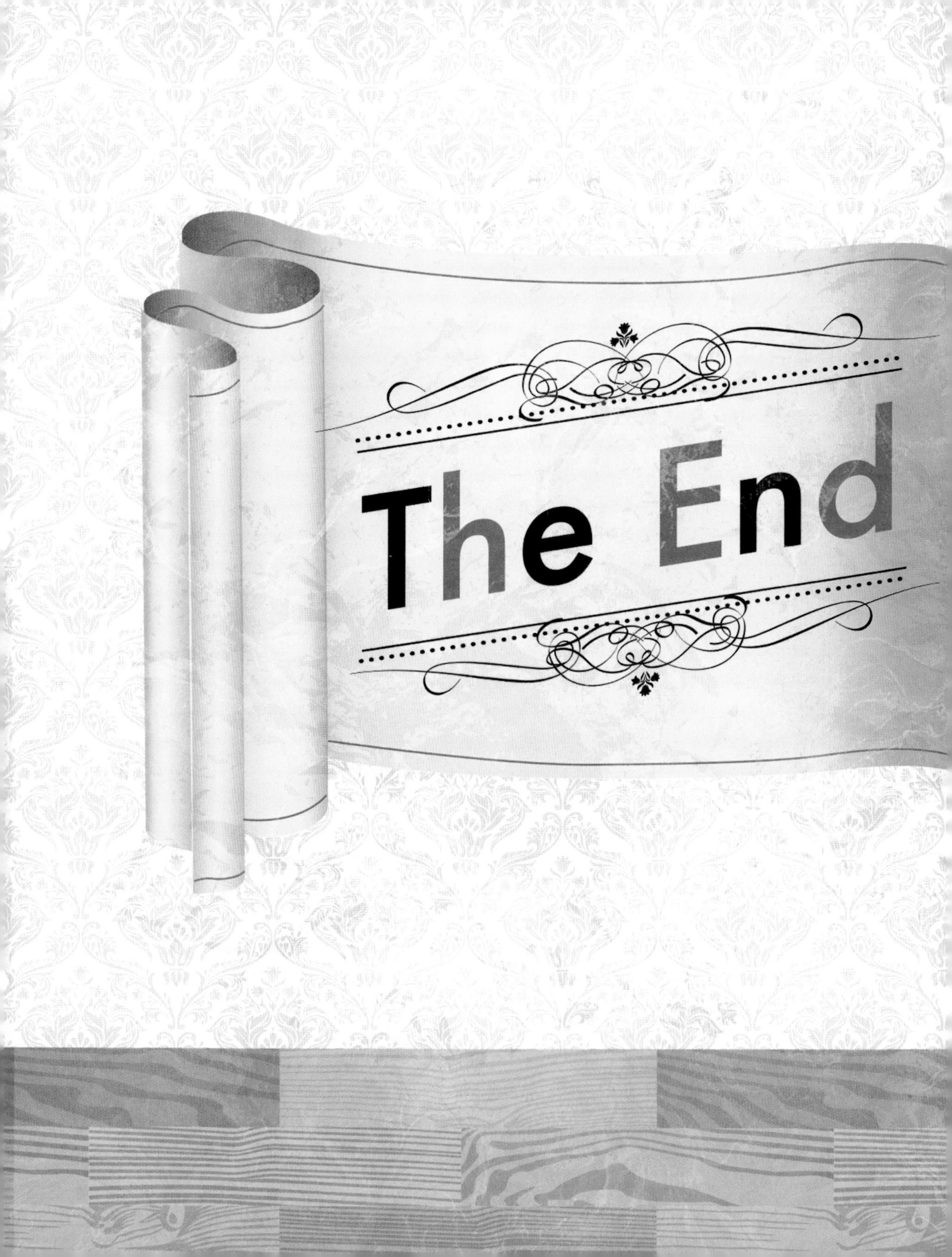
The End

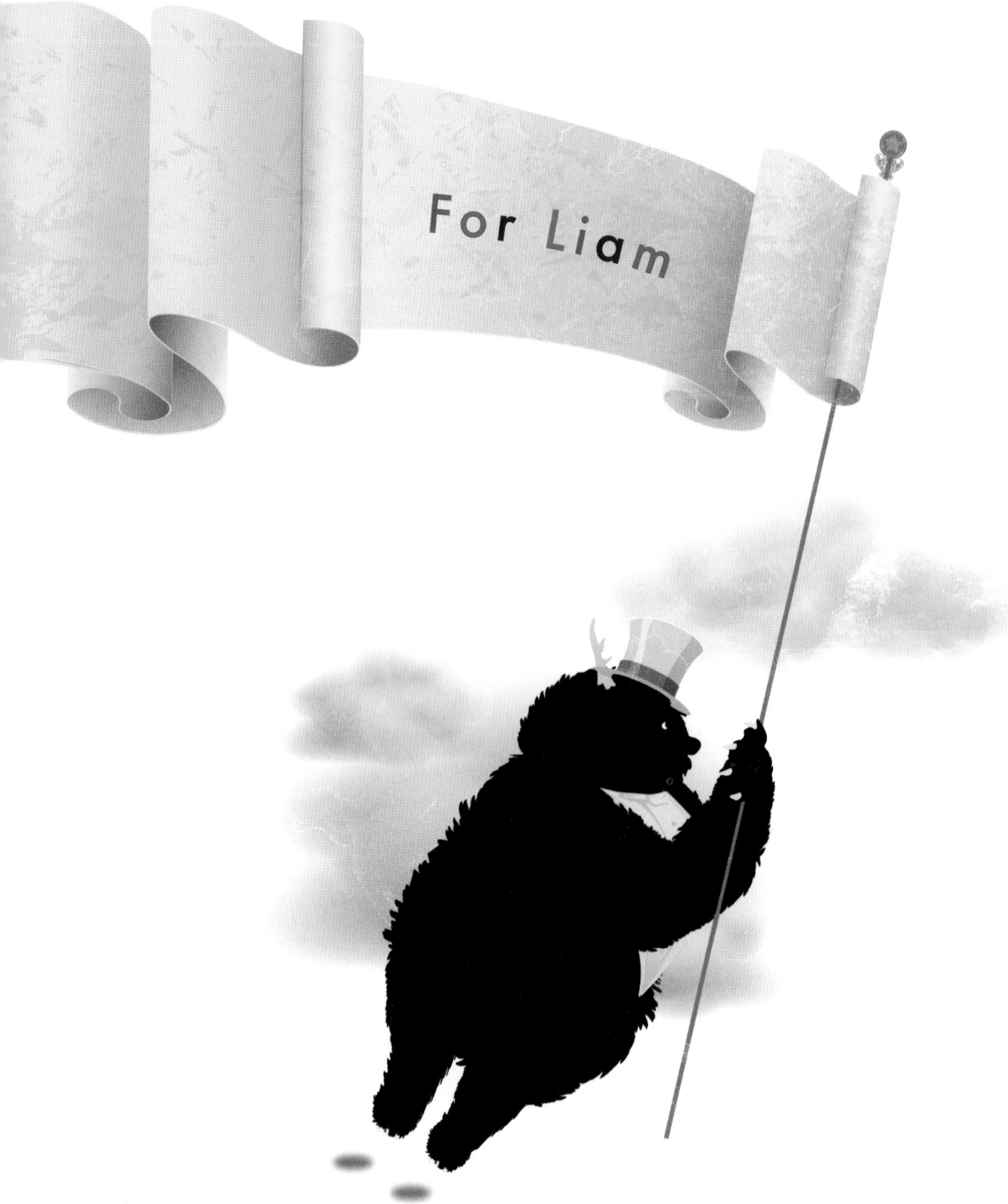
For Liam